DRAGONS WITHIN
Guarding Her Own

Other Books in the

Dragons Within

Anthology Series

Dragons Within: Claiming Her Wings

Dragons Within: Embracing Her Fire

DRAGONS WITHIN

Guarding Her Own

BALANCE OF SEVEN

Dallas

For information, contact:
Balance of Seven, www.balanceofseven.com
Publisher: dyfreeman@balanceofseven.com
Managing Editor: tntinker@balanceofseven.com

Cover Design: Eben Schumacher Art, ebenschumacherart.artstation.com

Copyediting and Formatting: TNT Editing, www.theodorentinker.com/TNTEditing

Publisher's Cataloging-in-Publication Data

Title: Dragons within : guarding her own / Balance of Seven.
Description: Dallas, TX : Balance of Seven, 2019. | Series: Dragons within; book 2. | Contents: Fire Dance / Finn O'Malley – Last Scion / Leo Otherland – Rebirth / Celosia Crane – Fire Legacy / Hayley Green – Riding the Lightning / Jess Reece – Makara's Treasure / Kimberly Gail – Scorpions of Justice / Shannon McRoberts – Burned Out / Amanda Mills Woodlee – My Pukís / D. Marie Prokop – Branka's Shells / Kristine Haecker – Mine / Theda Vallee – The Art of Courage / Deana Rose Wilson. | Summary: Twelve stories feature strong women with dragon-like traits who pledge their lives to guard their own.
Identifiers: LCCN 2019953257 | ISBN 9781947012820 (pbk.) | ISBN 9781947012004 (ebook)
Subjects: LCSH: Character – Fiction. | Dragons – Fiction. | Women in literature. | Fantasy fiction. | Short stories. | BISAC: FICTION / Fantasy / Action & Adventure. | FICTION / Fantasy / Dragons & Mythical Creatures.| FICTION / Women.
Classification: LCC PS509.F3 D73G 2019 (print) | PS509.F3 (ebook) | DDC 813 D73G--dc23
LC record available at https://lccn.loc.gov/2019953257

25 24 23 22 21 20 19   1 2 3 4 5

To those who have found their dragons within:

may your freedom and strength

support your fight

to protect what you believe in.

Contents

Introduction

Dear Reader, human or otherwise,

Dragons have been part of my life for as long as I can remember. They swooped in from the skies of Anne McCaffrey's Pern, the seas of Naomi Novik's fantastical England, and the Isle of Berk. They settled around me in the form of brilliant statuettes and wondrous illustrations. They sank into my soul, inviting me to accept myself as one of their own.

Over the years, my understanding of my dragon within has evolved. With the quiet fire of my imagination, my wings of escapism, and the scales I hide behind emotionally, I once believed that my dragon within was not meant for the real world but only to flourish in stories, mine or others.

Now, though I still love to escape into stories, I've found a new meaning for my dragon within: protection.

As a storyteller, I have always been protective of my own stories, worlds, and other imaginings. But in the years since I became an editor, that protection has unfurled to include so much more: the stories of the authors whose works I edit, and the dreams of the writers I watch grow and thrive.

Introduction

Twelve of these writers have found their way into these pages, claiming their dragons within and guarding fiercely that which means the most to them: their dreams, their hearts, and their values.

Now, dear reader, we present our hoard of tales to you. We invite you to dive in with arms spread wide and the belief that, even in words, a dragon's protection is strong and true.

Theodore Niretac Tinker
Managing Editor,
    Balance of Seven
Leader, Creative Central

fIRE DANCE

Finn O'Malley

'm gonna need to see some ID." The overweight man at the entrance of the club grunted the words over the blaring music drifting out the door.

Hand to her ear, the petite woman trying to get in scowled. "What?"

"ID," he repeated, annoyance trailing through his pronunciation. "If you want in, ya gotta show me you're over twenty-one." He leaned on the podium with such force, she thought it might break beneath his excessive weight.

"I need to get in." She shoved strands of her fiery-red hair behind her ears, slamming her teeth together in frustration.

"I ain't lettin' ya in without ID." He dismissed her presence, glancing past her. "Next!"

"Aw, come on, Tank. Let her in. She's cute."

The man behind her shoved forward, resting his arm across her shoulders. Immediately shrugging off his offensive touch, she consciously decided *not* to elbow him in the ribs. Percy met the beady eyes of the heavyset doorman, apparently named Tank. His gaze bounced between her and the eager man beside her. He glared for a long breath debating before nodding her through.

Tank will probably die soon.

She shook off the prophetic thought from her gifts and focused on her purpose for being in this realm: finding the sigil. However, her movement was halted as something grabbed her hand and pulled her backward.

"Hey, hey, where ya goin'?" Arm-boy gave Percy a pouty smile as glazed brown eyes perused her small frame. He had been drinking; the stench permeated his body. Amber eyes narrowed as she shook off his grasp.

"Do you want to die?" The question sent him flinching backward.

"All right, all right." He put his hands up. "Bitch."

She didn't understand why the word held offense here, but her response was immediate. She stepped forward, grabbing his shirt. In the center of his chest, sharp fingernails bit through the thin material, piercing his delicate flesh.

"What the . . ." His eyes darted around as fear jumped into his face.

"You should be nicer to the women of your realm." Her small, five-foot frame overpowered him with such force, he stumbled backward. Head ticking to the right, she concentrated on the beat of the heart under her grip.

Thump, thump, thump.

Releasing her breath, she closed her eyes and paused for the quickest moment. Humans such as this one, with his overt innuendos, pressed on her limited patience. In her realm, women were respected and admired for their wisdom and gifts. She struggled with the vast differences she often encountered while in the Earth realm. Releasing him with resignation, she turned on her heel.

The sigil.

She knew it was here. Magic pulsed in waves through the disgusting club, infiltrating her acute senses. Trying to keep her focus, she brushed past jackets tossed over the backs of chairs scattered around small tables, weaving her way toward the sign that read *Restrooms.* A brief survey of the hallway revealed two restroom doors and another door with a sign reading *Private.*

There.

Leaning against the wall of the hallway, she kicked one chunky combat boot up underneath her, pretending to tie her shoe. Percy had trained diligently in the art of deception, and she would need every skill available to retrieve the artifact.

When she was chosen by the coven, she had known the job would be difficult. Several witches had already failed, in part because the job required a unique set of skills. Her skills. Skills that marked her as a misfit among witches. Skills she had learned growing up in a family of bounty hunters. The Triquetra might have claimed her as a member of their coven, but they still employed her as a bounty hunter.

"Are you in line?" A thin brunette pointed to the restroom, interrupting her survey of the hall.

"No." Percy allowed the woman to pass into the line of miniskirts. She didn't understand the culture in this realm, the half-naked bodies writhing to attract a mate. As the brunette settled in to wait, she turned back to Percy with a curious stare.

Percy pretended to peer at her nails as she observed the door marked *Private*. With her hair shadowing her face, she closed her eyes and used her magical gifts to examine the room behind the door. Within her mind, she could sense him—Lorcan, the owner of the club—sitting behind a desk. The sigil seemed to be contained within a lockbox set in the wall. Magical protections layered the door and surrounded the lockbox, arcs of magic looping through the realm.

Bloody goddess above.

This would take some finesse. He must have been aware that the coven was after the sigil; this particular usage of linking spells hinted at a high level of fear regarding security. She pulled back slowly to not give away her presence within his magic.

The door swung open.

"Persephone," a gravelly voice called out to her. Poking her tongue into her cheek, she rolled her eyes and pushed off the wall, strolling into the room. "I thought you were better than that." The man within had his feet kicked up on the corner of the desk as he shuffled a deck of cards.

Percy glared and stopped just inside the doorway, crossing her arms. She'd underestimated his use of protection magic and chided herself for breaking his shadow charms. She *did* know better. The man paused in his shuffling and flicked two fingers, slamming the door closed behind her.

"Lorcan," Percy acknowledged with raised eyebrows. "I thought you were doing some dirty work for Viego back in our realm."

"Well, one must diversify." He tossed several cards into the air. Onyx eyes met hers as the cards hung in midair, rotating in place, first their fronts facing her, then their decorative red backsides. Around them, protection magic rippled through the room, ebony threads looping symbols of dark enchantment against the walls, their magical presence gleaming in her sight. The witch in her wanted to break them, to destroy his use of illegal magic.

"What brings me the pleasure of seeing you in this realm?" The cards moved through the air now, and with a small gesture of his eyes, Lorcan shifted them in a floating spiral. A warning of his telekinetic powers.

"You have something that doesn't belong to you." She made her way toward his desk, her left hand drawing blue spirals through the symbols on the wall. His lips pressed together as her magic caused discord through his spells.

"I have lots of things," he challenged.

"You know of what I speak, Lorcan." She traced a finger across his desk, gouging deeply into the wood. His jaw muscles twitched, and a smirk danced over her lips.

"Perhaps we can make a deal," he offered, rubbing a hand through his dark hair. The acrid fragrance of lies and deception assaulted her, and she huffed out a breath.

"How about you make this easy on me and just give me what I want?" She wished for the shortest moment that he would do as she asked, but it wouldn't be that kind of night. Incapable of *deals*, Lorcan was the epitome of Dark, and she chased Dark for a living. Besides, taking what she had come for would be more fun. She winked at him and turned, walking to the wall on her right.

As she stood in front of an ugly image of dogs playing poker, the lockbox revealed itself in her mind's eye. She peered back over her shoulder at Lorcan. Threads of deep red swirled from his fingertips as he contemplated her. His blatant use of magic in the Earth realm disturbed her, even if there weren't any humans around to see.

"Who hired you, Persephone?"

The threads turned into a flame that flickered above his palm. Eyeing him, she moved to the chair in front of his desk and sat down, kicking up her feet. Leather jacket splayed around her, she pulled out one of her karambits. Her weapon of choice, the curved double-edged blade resembled a claw. Its use was so instinctive for her that it might as well have been an extension of her hand.

Unhappy with the repetitive use of her full name, Percy frowned and twirled the curved blade by the finger ring at the end of the handle. "Why does it matter?"

"I would like to know who sent one of Magic's best hunters after me." He casually flipped the ball of flame across the cards that still hung in midair, igniting them one after the other.

A wicked smile crossed Percy's mouth. "The best," she affirmed. Her bloodline of dragon and witch, as well as her unique code of protection, maintained her status as one of the most coveted magical bounty hunters, particularly now that she was part of the Triquetra Coven.

"We will see, won't we?" Lorcan chucked the ball of fire in her direction, and she flipped her blade, rejecting the magic in a shower of light, instantaneously extinguishing his ball of red flames. The music inside the club shifted then, and its deep bass reverberated through the walls.

"Interesting place you have chosen." She spun her blade again. The club, Aces and Eights, was known for an assortment of illegal activities operating under the premise of a dance club: from drug running, to gambling, to something called stripping. Percy didn't want to know.

"Humans fascinate me. Their willingness to give themselves for the simplest of things . . ." He regarded her casual posture in the chair. "Money."

She gripped the handle of the knife, and her brows edged up.

"I didn't say they were the brightest, only that they fascinate me."

"So you use them and steal their power?" she asked. He disgusted her. He continued to break her rules in multiple directions; this really would be enjoyable.

He shrugged, smiling deviously. "So? They don't know."

The blade circled around her hand. "That doesn't make it okay; it makes you an asshole of the worst kind." She shifted in the chair, rocking forward.

"We all have our place."

Percy's eyebrows pinched together in a frown. She supposed there was a need for evil such as him because it gave her a job. Abruptly standing, she slammed her palm down on the desk. A ripple of blue unfurled down her arm, driving into Lorcan's boots, which rested on the corner of the desk. The magic sent him rolling back in his chair.

"Hey, that's not nice."

"I never said I was the nice type." Blue swirls danced around her body, ancient symbols unfurling in rapid progression as magic filled the room. The revealing spell spread in spirals of opalescent azure trails, searching his enchantments for any kind of irregularities. "Oh, Lorcan. You have deceived me." As her magic flowed through the room, breaking down his spells, she had found that the lockbox did not contain the sigil, but a magical counterfeit.

A sly smile slid across Lorcan's face. "I'm one of the best too."

"Hardly." She released the magic and folded her arms. A knock sounded at the door then, before it swung open.

"Hey, Boss, we got a problem in—" The voice cut off as Percy turned around.

Karambits spinning in both hands, Percy let shards of sapphire light stream to the floor. If Lorcan used blatant magic in front of his men, she would too.

Lorcan's hand shot up to stop his man at the door. "Percy, I'm afraid I must end our little game here." Standing, he rested the tips of his fingers on the desk.

Percy's gaze bounced back and forth, ending up on Lorcan's man in the doorway. Glaring at her, he muttered something he probably believed would be indiscernible to her. However, with her keen supernatural hearing, she heard the "Triq trash" comment with precise clarity. Her hand twitched uncontrollably, but she immediately rejected the idea of enveloping him in a torture spell as he turned to leave the room. Sometimes, protecting humans—even ones like this—was exceedingly difficult.

"I have things to attend to." Lorcan came around the desk. He clasped her arm, pulling her toward the door. Percy's teeth set, grinding against each other, before she wrenched her body away from his hold, irritated by the closeness of his form.

"You won't be retrieving the sigil tonight." With a flourishing bow, he begged her through the door. While it might have been a gesture of kindness for some, the look on his snide face said that, from him, it was a gesture of smugness. He thought he had outmaneuvered her.

Let him think that.

His limited interactions with Percy had made him overconfident and cocky, which would only play to her advantage. Instead of protesting, she busied herself with searching for the sigil in her mind. Regaining a firm grasp on the crook of her elbow, Lorcan dragged her onto the main floor of the club while she searched past the distractions.

It must be here, she thought. *Somewhere, but where?*

Momentarily struck by smoky air, thumping music, and more bodies crammed into a small space than seemed humanly possible, she shook off Lorcan's grasp. The mass of sweaty and scantily dressed bodies moved in a wave that matched the pulse of the deep bass, all turned to face the elevated stage where the DJ stood like a messiah of music.

In her mind's eye, the club layout unfolded: the main dance floor in front of her with the DJ to the left, the bar straight ahead through the mass of people, and tucked between the bar and the DJ, another door leading to the basement level. That must have been where most of the illegal activities occurred. There were several rooms down a long hallway, some layered in magic, others not.

Interesting. Percy had to give him credit; Lorcan wasn't making this easy on her.

There! Just the slightest flutter of power.

"Don't make me escort you out of here, Perce." Lorcan held his hands out to the sides as if he were trying to be the nice guy. "Why don't you have a drink on me, maybe get laid? You look like you could use it," he called over the music with a wave of one hand as he disappeared into the crowd of bodies on the dance floor.

Streams of colorful light pulsated with the music, illuminating the club in hazy loops of color. Percy's eyes narrowed and the corners of her lips turned up as she navigated through the throng of humans, pushing her way to the hidden door where Lorcan had disappeared. With a quick glance around to make sure no one was watching, she waved her hand over the door, magically forcing it open. On the other side was a long hallway with another door at the end, presumably leading to the stairs. Standing in front of the other door and blocking her way was the man who had interrupted her in Lorcan's office.

"You shouldn't be in here," he declared, crossing his heavy arms over his chest.

She grinned. "I'm always where I shouldn't be." She flipped out her spelled karambits, spinning them in her grip. Magic trailed off them in spirals of greens and blues, and the man's eyes widened. "You have no idea who I am. If you did, you would be running down the hall."

She observed the fear ticking across his face, but he stood still, apparently refusing to lose face against a five-foot-tall woman. Lines of magic whirled between them as she stepped closer.

"Last chance." Percy's smile was wicked as the spell began. With an agile step forward, she raised her leg in a spin kick, blasting the magic through the hallway. The man flew backward, landing with a heavy thud against the door to the stairs. Percy pushed her boot into his chest and leaned down.

"What was that you muttered before? Something about Triq trash?"

His face ashen, he tried to speak, but he was locked in a spiral of terror and the words stuck.

"I didn't think so." Her foot ground into his sternum, causing the breath to heave out of his lungs in sputters. "Triqs aren't for kids or lowlife scum like you, Li'l Bub." The use of his nickname sent a new flare of fear through him as he tried to escape her hold.

With a flash of her hand, a glittery sand fell over his face, knocking him unconscious. He would spend the next few hours trapped in torturous nightmares, eaten by insects and whatever else his subconscious decided. She mildly regretted using the spell she had gained from the Air Faeries, wishing instead that she could be the one to torture him. Leaving him to his slumber, she opened the door, letting his head clunk against the hard floor. She strode down the stairs and deeper into the club.

Magic pulsed from the far end of the hall: Lorcan and the sigil, together. *Convenient.* Two more men stood outside the door, which shimmered with black and gold lines of dark enchantments. The swirls and patterns overlapped one another in layers of protection, beckoning her to break them. Percy could easily teleport into the room, past the protections, but this way would be far more entertaining. Firm, suspicious faces turned toward her, and she waved.

"What the hell are you doing down here?" yelled a goateed man.

"I'm lost. Please, help me!" Percy feigned with a snicker. Goatee shifted his weight before pointing back toward the stairs.

"Get out of here. Back upstairs," Blockhead growled from next to Goatee.

Was she five? Jeez. Closer now, she slammed her elbow into the side of Goatee's face, to which Blockhead pulled a 9 mm and stuck the barrel in her face. Percy swung around, bringing her elbow down on his wrist, and the gun fell from his hand. Capturing it midfall, she popped the clip, unchambered the round, and tossed it down the hall.

"I don't like guns."

Percy smashed the heel of her hand into Blockhead's chest, and indigo ripples of magic convulsed through his chest, shooting him backward. The magic held him against the wall. Both hands outstretched, she allowed her power to swirl and concentrated on expanding the spell.

Before she could finish, Goatee grabbed her leg from his position on the floor. Tilting her head in annoyance, she radiated fire magic through her leg and into his hand. He screamed out in pain and let go quickly, clutching at the internal burning that seethed under his skin.

So much for surprising Lorcan.

A fast flare from her hands silenced the sound of his cries. Waving her hand at the lock on the door, she left the two men incapacitated on the floor.

Opening the door, Percy didn't know what to expect, but the flashy high-roller poker game she found had her raising her eyebrows. Standing next to the dealer, Lorcan glanced up and his mouth became a heavy line upon seeing her.

"Percy, I told you no."

The players half glanced in her direction, staying focused on their cards. The power of the sigil emanated from the pocket of Lorcan's casual suit jacket, giving Percy pause.

He had had the artifact all along? *How did he do that?*

"No isn't really an acceptable answer for me." She cocked a hip and folded her arms. "All right, game's over," she said to the players. Faces turned to her in agitation before looking to Lorcan.

"Please, gentlemen, if you would allow me to take care of this . . ." Lorcan offered the players an apologetic smile.

One of the men's bodyguards took a step toward Percy. Without hesitation, she kicked out her foot, knocking him off-balance. As he stumbled, she elbowed him in the shoulder, causing him to collapse onto the lush, dark carpet. The prone man tried to come up again, but she placed her boot on his back, restricting his movement.

"Stay." Her foot dug in with pressure he wouldn't have expected. Terrified human eyes turned in her direction, and cards were folded against the table in anticipation. "This is where you leave."

The sharp sound of chairs being pushed away from the table filled the room as the players retreated in cautious fear, leaving the cards dispersed across the table in chaos. She nudged the bodyguard at her feet. "You too." The bodyguard scrambled to the door.

"Persephone." Lorcan's gaze flicked upward as he walked toward her.

"Can you *please* just give me the sigil?" Her eyes fluttered closed, and she called on the goddess to give her patience as he had used her full name, *again.*

A ball of fire erupted to life on his palm. "You have already cost me a poker game. You need to leave."

"Cute. You think fire scares me?" Advancing swiftly, Percy turned her side to him and kicked him in the sternum, forcing him backward several steps. The fireball ricocheted haphazardly off the wall to her left. "Dragon blood runs through my veins. I am made of fire."

Hunched low, he tried charging forward, but she quickly stepped aside. As he passed, she elbowed him in the soft spot behind his ear, sending him to his hands and knees with a grunt of pain.

"I asked nicely before: give me the damn stone." Percy extended her open palm in front of his face. She could feel the anger building inside him, but she didn't expect him to slam the back of his right arm into the side of her leg, nearly knocking her over. She regained her balance with a swift movement and looped her arm around the one he had struck her with, holding it back at an awkward angle. Wrenching him upright, she forced him to bobble precariously on his knees as his left hand flew out to the side to help him keep his balance.

"Seriously?" She pulled his arm back tighter, offering her hand again. "Are you done yet?"

Lorcan twisted his body against her, tugging to escape her ferocious hold, even as he tried to create another ball of flames. Percy grabbed her karambit and flipped it to dissipate his half-formed magic, sending out a spurt of blue light that seared the floor beneath him. Swirling the curved blade around her finger, she hooked the tip into the corner of his mouth.

Lorcan instantly stilled, not daring to even flinch against the razor-sharp steel. With a slow purposeful movement, he reached his free hand into his jacket to retrieve the sigil.

Magic glistened within an orb of brilliant light. Shimmers of ethereal blues sizzled from the artifact, and Percy's eyes dilated beneath the beautiful pulsing. Silky obsidian smooth within her palm, the Triquetrum Stone was finally in her possession.

A few months ago, the coven seer had a vision, revealing an impending peril that would devastate the coven and the future of magic. The priestess required the stone for a concealment spell, to change the course of the vision and protect a future witch. Perhaps retrieving the sigil would finally prove Percy's worth to the other witches, at last winning her their favor.

"Now was that so hard?" she asked, releasing Lorcan's arm with a fling, letting the momentum totter him forward to almost land on his face. Sliding the stone into her pocket, she felt the cool undulations pulsate against her body.

"I think I'll take that drink now," she said.

Lorcan wiped the back of his hand across his mouth, smearing the blood on his lip. Opening his mouth to speak, he stopped short when she arched her brow. Rapidly assessing his current predicament, he debated his choices. Entertained, she smiled.

Then he disappeared.

Coward.

Straightening her jacket with a small tug, she headed back upstairs, past the defeated, unconscious bodies of Lorcan's men. The deafening music and sweaty bodies attacked her sensitive abilities as she pushed open the door to the main floor. After wading through people along the perimeter of the room, Percy stopped by the bar, signaling for a drink. A woman with amethyst hair leaned across the bar.

"What can I get for you?" she half yelled. Percy gave her half a glance as she turned toward the DJ, whose red headphones bobbed to the sway of music.

"Something strong," she called back. When the shot glass appeared, she returned her gaze to the purple-haired bartender and met the predatory gleam of vampire eyes.

Lorcan employed vampires?

Head cocked, she tracked the vampire as she moved down the bar, helping innocent humans with drinks. Turmoil raced through Percy. Her only assignment had been to retrieve the sigil. Not to save humans. Not to interfere with Lorcan's obvious issues with magical ordinances. Although this kind of thing usually fell under the coven's responsibilities, protocol required her to report back to the priestess before any decisions could be made.

Perhaps the vampire had needed a job? Shrugging it off, she tried to excuse the behavior, slamming back the shot of burning liquid and setting the glass back on the bar.

The inner debate raging through her reached its tipping point when the purple-haired bloodsucker stretched over the bar to kiss a thin brunette female. The same woman who had watched Percy curiously from the bathroom line. The vampire whispered something in her ear, making the brunette laugh.

Eyes drifting closed for the shortest moment, Percy tried to breathe, but her own personal code as a witch, fused with that of her dragon blood, screamed in her mind. Leaving humans to Lorcan's disposal, that of his club, or vampires was unacceptable to her, and to the coven. The Triquetra would interfere eventually, as they were the force for upholding human safety against all magical existence.

But *eventually* wasn't fast enough for Percy. This was where she and the coven differed. Why shouldn't she just solve the problem now?

Reaching across the bar, she grabbed a full bottle and poured herself another shot. Bound by her own set of rules, she made the decision to burn the place down. The favor she would earn for retrieving the stone might not be enough after this.

Swallowing the shot, she snapped the glass down on the bar, and with it, flames ignited across the bottles. The alcohol, mixed with her magic, became a rapid accelerator for the flames, which soon licked up the wall.

Sharp, desperate screams saturated the air. Percy leaned against the bar patiently, unbothered by the oppressive heat of the flames behind her. Pouring herself another shot, she casually observed as the swarm of people moved in a new direction of scattered chaos, racing out the front doors. As the club emptied, she monitored the doors to make sure every human was accounted for, before casting a quick spell to protect any unknown humans downstairs. Not one single innocent would be harmed under her watch, on any assignment, especially this one. The Triquetra guarded their own, and the humans of this realm were bound beneath their protection.

In a slow stride, Percy walked to the exit, allowing the flames of her blood to consume everything behind her in a blaze of destruction.

Outside, the cool air washed away Percy's remaining frustration as the sound of sirens careened closer. The horde of humans stood in a cluster, watching the building burn. She slipped by them, concealed in a spell of shadows. She removed the Triquetrum from her jacket, and the sharp angles of the deep black stone reflected the flames behind her as the fire raged.

"I should have charged double."

Last Scion

Leo Otherland

Hatchling

The dragons had died years before. Or so the stories said. All I knew of the genocide that destroyed my home and ended my kin came to me in dreams. I was still in the shell when it happened; my sire had hidden me in the earth for protection while she went out to fight. By the time my shell imploded to become the core of my beating heart, my home had already become a cold thing, lain waste some twenty years before.

From the dreams in my shell, I knew Dragon Foundry to be a nature altar, one of the great beacons the gods had built by magic at the birth of the world. An ornate fortress on a green hill, it guarded the altar stone within. In our possessive natures, we dragons hoarded the offerings of the younger races and passed to them the stories of time.

By the time I clawed my way out of the earth to take my first breath, though, my home was nothing more than a ruin of tumbled, moss-covered stone on a barren, rocky hill. Its fire out, Dragon Foundry was as dead as its denizens.

As a naked newborn, I wandered the wreck, looking at the dust that had been my fellows and wondering which it was who had borne me. But my sire was gone with the rest, and I could not tell her from the others.

I went to the altar stone. It was broken, split in two and desecrated with long, lashing scars. I howled my despair to the iron sky and curled into the wedge of space created by the altar stone's two halves. I wanted to mourn my kin and my sire, but I knew them not yet and mourned for myself, that I was alone. For some while, I wanted to die, but after several weeks of raging and weeping and dreaming, I wanted another thing. For that, I needed life.

Luckily, it was easy to live, for dragons were born fully grown, with the wisdom of ages and a thousand times a thousand stories in their core.

Starving and weak, I crawled out of Dragon Foundry. The lands around were wild and open. They were filled with rabbits, voles, and edible plants and roots that I did not scorn digging my fingers far enough into the earth to find. I gorged myself that first day I chose to live, before returning to Dragon Foundry to dream.

Dragons did not dream as other races did. When dragons dreamed, we dreamed of the truth of what had come before in the world. It was our gift as lore keepers. As the last living dragon, it was my place to dream of the end of my kin.

By night, I dreamed of the army of man that had dragged itself to Dragon Foundry. Of the catapults, ballistae, and siege engines they had used to break it. Of how they had robbed and defiled. And of a king in an iron crown who had dug the cores from the hearts of my sisters and shattered the altar stone in two with a great hammer.

By day, I dreamed another dream. One of fury and vengeance.

The land about the wreck of my home was primarily waste, but there were some human settlements clinging like precarious moss to the rocks. Like a wild animal, I stalked down among them, but the humans I found there were not the steel-and-leather-clad men and women who had ended my kind. These were nothing but weary, rag-covered creatures, struggling to eke out an existence under a sunless sky, on ground which had turned against them. These I could pity—even if I did do a small amount of pillaging.

Though dragons held magic and were forces of nature incarnate, we were born in the bodies of the younger races. Frail-looking frames of soft flesh, which need to be clothed, warmed, and fed, covered our true forms like thin veils. These humans possessed things I needed if I were to care for my outer form.

After I had washed in a stream, I dressed myself in the rough fabric and leather boots I had acquired, twisted my ash-gray hair into dreadlocks, and hunted the lands surrounding Dragon Foundry to sate my hunger and bloodlust. My white-on-white eyes (*blind-white eyes*—iris, pupil, and sclera all the same continuous color, like an obscenity against my dusky skin) missing nothing of what passed.

The land had become desolate with the breaking of the nature altar and the extinguishing of the beacon, a great heatless flame that had swirled upward from the altar stone. The blessings of the gods and all magic had drained away. This, I had no desire to remedy. *This,* I would not repair until I was appeased. This, I *would not* alter until humankind repented its assault on nature itself.

Yet I was dragon. I was born a guardian of the younger children of the earth, so neither could I ignore the suffering of the humans in their settlements. I returned to them with gifts of game and what healing I could provide to man and cattle. I showed the humans what plants remained edible and which had turned poisonous, which crops would still grow and what would wither.

And I told them stories and received their offerings to the gods.

I had allowed them to see my true form. Knowing me for what I was, they honored and blessed me and allowed me to come and go among them as I pleased. For a time, though I was neither satisfied nor at peace within myself, I remained at least fulfilled in the completion of my natural responsibilities.

This was not to last for long.

I had not considered what revealing myself to man would bring.

Storyteller

It was my sharp eyes that alerted me. I saw them long before they had climbed halfway to my perch. I knelt on a great slab of gray-green stone pointing out over the brow of the hill, taking in a view of the broken road below. My hands were locked around the rough edge of the stone, and my face turned into the wind, which tugged at my hair and whiffed their scent up to me. There were five coming toward me. Humans. Two female, three male. They had left their horses at the base of the hill and toiled upward on foot. I could have hunted them easily, but I wanted to know what they were about, so I hid myself to watch.

Once the humans had labored to the summit, they searched the remnants of Dragon Foundry, four of them aiding and guarding the fifth. I watched them enter what remained of the great foyer and watched as they took in the tumbled stones and glittering shivered shards of glass. I followed them as they climbed the remains of the now-twisted and crumbling towers and descended back to the emptied hoards. I crept after as they entered the inner sanctuary of uprooted standing stones, where the altar stone lay in the center. Though I was always close, they found nothing to betray I was there, and they returned to the stone I had knelt on as I tracked their initial approach.

"There is nothing here, my lady," one of the men said. "Nothing to show that a dragon haunts this place. The rumor circulating through the holds has proven to be only that." His voice softened. "The queen will be pleased you did all you could. Especially in lending aid to her subjects."

"Yes, she will be pleased," repeated the object of the former's words. But she did not seem pleased. Rather, her words were sad. She was a small thing with silken hair. A white scar bisected one milky blind eye, which had most likely held color before injury claimed its ability of sight. Another scar ran from her ear to her jaw.

Though she wore chain mail and a sword on one hip, her left arm hung limp and dead, bound to her in a sling. "Let us go."

Her companions turned away, but the scarred one lingered a moment more, as if branding the ruins upon her memory.

"My lady? Are you well?"

"Yes. I am coming." Her eye roamed over my place of concealment, flickered, and moved on. Then she was gone, beginning the long descent.

The humans left, but not alone. I followed, the possibility of revenge for my kin and peace for my own tumultuous being at last laid before me. In my mind, a true plan had been born. I would have the king who had laid low my kind and kin.

I let them remount their horses and slough on for several hard miles before I appeared above them on a hilltop. I simply stood from the rough grass turf and stones where I had lain on my belly, watching. They reined in their horses, startled, the four guards pulling swords and shouting.

"Who are you? Speak!"

I only sat down, one leg cocked, arm braced on knee, and a grin pulling back from my sharp teeth.

"Curse you!" the man who had spoken at Dragon Foundry flung at me. "What are you?" Obviously, I was not merely human. A glance would have been enough to show them this. Not only were my teeth strange. My whole aura would be odd, the force of my white-on-white eyes frightening.

"Be still, Cel'burn," the scarred woman said. "There is no need to assault an unarmed woman alone in the wild." She urged her horse forward a few paces before reining it in and turning her single eye up toward me, good arm braced on her saddle horn. "I am the Lady Lor, the Queen's Right Hand. Who are you who travels the waste?"

My grin pulled wider. "I am Quinn." With a quick and singular motion, I slithered down the hillside in a slide of loose rocks and shale to stand before them. Despite the lady's words, her guardians gripped their weapons tighter at my approach. I paid them no mind. With a bow, I said, "I am a wandering *shribner*, or so we storytellers of the old way were once called. I noted your passing and followed in hope of listeners."

"A blind *shribner*," the lady mused. "You must have been taught by a dragon."

I spread my arms, inviting her to take me in. "I am too young for that. And I am not blind," I added as an afterthought. "I was taught by a man who was taught by a dragon. If you allow me to accompany you to the royal court, I will spin you tales greater than any you have ever heard."

"If you are not blind, you must have magic," Lor mused.

Because there must be some explanation for my strangeness. I knew they must be thinking this, and as it was said, magic altered all. Nothing could be touched by magic and remain the same.

My grin flared, and I spread my arms again. "A little, Lady Lor."

"Stories and magic are good to have as one travels." Her eye, watching me with such steadiness, flickered as it had in Dragon Foundry. For a moment, I was unnerved, wondering if she knew me. Yet she went on as if she did not. "Especially under these perpetual clouds. You may come with us."

"My lady!" Cel'burn protested. "Are you sure this is wise? We know nothing of her!" The last words were fierce.

"If I were wise, perhaps I would have been dead long ago," Lor responded, calm. To me, she said, "Come, Quinn. We have long leagues, which will stretch to weeks, before we reach the queen's court."

My grin flashed haughtily as I took up position beside the lady's horse. It was apparent Cel'burn and the other three were not pleased, but they put away their weapons.

We carried on through a landscape that alternated between barren moor and rolling shale-covered hills. All of it lay under a sky filled with scudding gray clouds, which had not dispersed since the light of Dragon Foundry went out. As I walked with the humans, I wove for them tales of gods and heroes, royals and commoners, elder races and fiends from the time before time, all while using magic to give them brief glimpses of slender, lither beauty, whiffs of scent, or the echo of far away bird song, hunting horn, or battle cry to enhance the words.

Gray fat, heavy rain fell on us ever and again as the day wore away. When the deepening shadows crept from under the cloud cover, the march stopped. The four guards pitched camp while I lit a turf fire with magic (a feat for which even Cel'burn was grudgingly grateful in the damp) and disappeared into the rocks for a short time. I returned with a collection of small game to char over the flames and share out. (Even dragons like their meat cooked.)

The lady then bid me to share her tent as her guards shared the other, earning further protest from Cel'burn (who appeared to speak for all on the matter). Lor brushed the protest aside with eternal surety. I aimed a feral smirk at the man as I ducked into the tent.

We sat, Lor and I, and I told her stories as she unbound her arm and unburdened herself of her armor.

"Enough of old stories," she said at last, face gray with old pain. "What of yourself, Quinn?"

"Myself?" I eyed her, wondering about the agonies she hid so well behind a careful face of calm without her tent. "I was born an orphan of the king's war. I learned my stories, and I tell them."

Lor nodded, massaging her left shoulder with her right fingers. After a moment, she gripped the left wrist and lifted the arm to cradle it in her lap.

"What of yourself?" I asked, white eyes narrowing. "What is that?" I indicated the useless arm where it lay. Someone had broken this woman in body as the king had broken my kin. My vengeance and possessiveness wished to know the *who*.

"An old battle injury." She sighed. "What of me? Let me see . . ." She shut her eyes, the living and the dead. "To tell you my story, I must tell you the queen's because I am the queen's aid. The old king wanted sons but only received one daughter." (I blinked. Dragons had but one sex, and I understood not mankind's need of a second or their glorification of one over the other if both were required.) "Because of this, she served as both daughter and son, learning war above the ways of womankind.

"The old king loved war and death and blood. He sent his conquering armies into all the nations around and razed them. He destroyed the dragons, incurring the wrath of the very elements, and why?" She opened her eye, its sandy gaze heavy. "Because they were free. Because they would not bow and swear fealty to a mortal king.

"The queen and I were like them. The dragons. We were free. We hated war. For a long while, we were too young to take action against the king, but we were not young always.

"There came a day when the queen heard her father meant to make war again, intended to send out his armies and ensnare another people who would not submit to his brutality. She deemed herself strong and her allies sure, and she defied him, rebelling against his rule. She challenged the king, and we two fought him together. Within the short space of a year, she had killed him with her own hand in combat and taken his throne.

"And I? I earned this." She gripped her dead arm with the living. "And the title of Right Hand.

"Since that time, the queen has walked the path of restitution. Returning lands that were stolen, freeing those enslaved, paying reparations where she can. But there are some things that cannot be amended. The dragons are gone, the altar at Dragon Foundry is broken with the beacon out, and there is no way to end this dreary blight upon the land but by some far chance." Her fist clenched. "Little grows these days, and man and beast starve. The ground itself is acid and crumbles away. I was sent to create reconciliation between nature and man, to atone for the sins of foolish mortals. I had hope when I went to Dragon Foundry, but now—"

She winced, rubbing at her shoulder again. Her pain was more apparent by the end of her rush of words and emotion.

I eyed her, my own internal mechanisms unwound by her narrative, my greed for vengeance shunted toward a new outcome. To this daughter of the iron-crowned king.

"Let me see it."

She did not refuse, instead baring the shoulder to me. And I saw, rage hardening in my core. A wide, spreading scar had been left by a sword that had aimed for the heart but had missed. It was no wonder the arm was useless. It was a wonder she had lived. I put my fingers on the scar, feeling it, easing the deep pangs of nerves cut by steel and infected with iron.

She exhaled in relief under my touch, sagging against me, and my eyes turned to hers. I moved my hand to her breast, and she made no protest. I pressed her to the ground, pushing harder at her breast, stealing her mouth with mine. She accepted my tongue with a groan, and we coupled there.

It was a thing we both needed. I felt, in the relaxing of the tensions within her, that it had been too long for both of us (for her before she was wounded, she admitted), and it was a thing of release only. I was dragon, and dragons needed no mates, except for pleasure. And, she? She was a woman mated already to her duty.

Yet a dragon's lust is matched by its greed. I had claimed her. She was *mine*, and the two following days were repetitions of the first. Days spent walking beside the plodding horses and telling stories, nights spent sharing her bed. Though on the first day after waking she articulated for me my understanding that what we were doing was nothing but a physical act, on the second night, as she drifted to sleep, she could not keep from revealing herself.

Dreamer

The revelation was poorly timed.

We had coupled after a day of walking through the weeping rain. The warmth and activity of our joining lulled me into a half sleep filled with true dreams while Lor was still awake. In my dream, I was my mother. The air of Dragon Foundry was acidic with smoke and metallic with blood. I/she stood before the altar stone in my/her frail humanoid body, placid and unmovable, pierced through the chest and abdomen with twin ballista bolts, bleeding iron poison into my/her blood even as my/her red life essence dripped and dribbled onto the ground. Outside the ring of standing stones was a king in an iron crown, his hammer braced upon the torn earth. Overhead, thunder rumbled in a dry, charged sky.

"Now, dragon, you will die," the king said, dragging his hammer from the earth.

My/her lips (my *mother's* lips) twitched into a smile, glinting sharp teeth. "You may kill me, human, but the lightning will still strike!" I/she snapped my/her teeth over the last word, raising hands to a sky blooming with clouds like blood from a wound. I/she lifted my/her face to receive the first swollen raindrop and was riven, smote down by the force of a hammer that would soon smite the altar stone in two.

I came fully awake with an angry hiss on my lips to find Lor curled beside me, lost in the unknowing place between dream and waking. Understanding not in the least what I had dreamed or my mood, Lor reached for me, knowing only I had stirred.

"Forgive me," she murmured, eyes closed. "I have lied. I am not Lor the Right Hand; I am Lor the queen. I have had need to be careful, as some do not approve my position of restoration. Forgive," she whispered a second time as she submitted to sleep. My eyes narrowed, and I plotted my vengeance, my mother's death fresh in my mind.

I pushed away from her and out into the starless night sky. So she had lied to me, the deceiver. It mattered not. She had ended her own lie, and I knew in an instant that my plan of following her back to the royal court would be needless and pointless all together. I could kill the ironclad queen at any moment. I shared her bed, and she lay there so heedless of me, even as I raged in the unbroken dark.

With these thoughts, I crept back to the queen's side. She slept on, breathing softly. I considered how I could crush out her life without breaking her sleep but found I could not. I was *dragon*. I was proud. I would allow her this: she would face her death with open eyes in the light of day.

I lay sleepless in her tent until the sun walked the ways of the sky above the clouds, and I ate little before camp was broken. As the day wore on, rain swept over us time and again, soaking us through. And I stalked her, this Queen Lor, awaiting the time I carved my retribution for my kin into her flesh. I envisioned her death as I walked beside her horse's flank in the gray morning. I rehearsed her last breath as we ate at sunless noon (feeling Cel'burn's eyes on me as though he knew my thoughts and intent).

But every time I came up behind her to sink my claws in, the dead arm in its sling would not allow me. My thoughts of blood were washed away by the words she had spoken to me in the tent.

This state persisted through the fall of the sun. I followed Lor into her tent that night but could not couple with her, so I prowled back out into camp once she had been subdued by sleep. I was growling to myself and envisioning blood when Cel'burn hailed me from the fire.

"Quinn. You have been having trouble sleeping these last few nights, storyteller."

I turned my eyes to the flaring embers and sparks. All of Lor's guards sat, arms braced on knees, around the dying fire, their own eyes hooded in the blended shadow-light. For a moment, I thought they knew my secret intent and meant their conclave to trap me, but then Cel'burn leaned back, turning his full face into the light and motioning to the place beside him.

"Come, join us. There is still some meat if you will have it."

There was no deceit in his face, so I slid into the place he indicated. "Have all of you troubled sleep as well?"

The woman shrugged. "For once, it is not raining. It is pleasant to sit by a fire and be dry."

I stared into the coals. "Why do you all follow the queen?" It was important to me, this understanding of such loyalty. From where had it come?

"Why?" The tone drew my gaze to Cel'burn. His voice *blazed.* "Look at us. We are not the queen's blood. We are all children of the conquered."

It was true. While Lor was all sand and beige (and the humans of the holds around Dragon Foundry had been brown as deep as the mud they tried to farm), Lor's guards were as various in shade as if no two were of the same kin.

"Look at me," Cel'burn repeated, indicating his skin and hair as white as wool. "I spent my childhood on the auction block. I was about to be sold again the day they carried Lor in from her last battle with the old king. Wounded as she was, the queen ordered her bearers to stop so she could declare slavery against the law and get me off that block. That day, I got down on my knees and swore I would follow her to the end of days, to fiery infinity and back."

There were murmurs of agreement all around. "Through death, to the end of all," the woman affirmed.

I turned my eyes back to the flames, considering my bent toward vengeance against Lor. Had I that right? Had I the desire to become the same kind of beast as the ironclad king, murdering indiscriminately?

Without further words, I got up and went back to Lor's tent. Within, she woke at my presence, curled around me, and attempted to kiss me. Holding her head, I asked, "Why do you do this?" I could not grasp it. Why spend her nights giving me her affections? There was no reason I could find for it within my own heart.

"Reconciliation," she said, looking into my eyes with her steady single-eyed gaze. "Did not my father destroy the *shribners* too? I will not follow in his steps."

With a growl, I coupled her. But my indecision lingered. I was torn within myself. I was uncertain what I wanted to do, until *humankind itself* offered me the answer.

Guardian

We had come out on another moorland, small and enclosed by hills, when a host—fifty or so armed and armored men and women— swept down upon us. It was neither sudden nor unbeknownst, at least not to me. I had felt the reverberations of their hoofbeats through the ground and scented their sweat and horses on the wind. I could have given warning, but even in my undone state, I wanted to see what these affairs of the metal clad would be. So I only stood by as they encircled us, bristling with steel. Their leader, a beige man with beige hair, beige skin, and washed out eyes, spoke from the fore.

"Now, queen, you will die."

Now, queen, you will die.

The words rang and stung in my ears, as the sight and scent of the ironclad humans stung my other senses. The armored men and women smelled metallic, of blood and steel, and their banner bore a great war hammer under an iron crown—the same banner that had hung on the war machines that ravaged my home. But Lor only sat on her horse, unmoving and unmoved. It was I who hissed and narrowed my eyes. Such words had been spoken to she who bore me. But not by *my* queen. Lor had never spoken words of murder and hate, yet they were given to her unreasonably.

"Well, have you nothing to say?" The taunt was followed by shifting laughter.

A cruel mirth that Lor's low voice silenced before Cel'burn's building venom could spill out. "You may kill me, sir, but what I have begun will not die."

More laughter followed these words. The beige man adjusted his seat in the saddle. "I find when you kill someone, their ideas die with them, as long as you kill those who share them. I will see to that after I have seen to you, Lor."

"You would not dare!" Cel'burn burst out.

"He would," Lor said softly. She eased her horse forward, passing her bodyguards. "It's what he feels I should have done to him and his followers after I defeated my father. The fact that I gave him leniency has only infuriated him all these years." To her assailant, she added, "If you must take a life, take mine and spare those who serve me. Please."

"My lady! No!"

"Be still, Cel'burn." Lor's eyes, the white and the sand, were only for the beige man.

It was too much. The queen waiting for the hammer strike.

I stepped out between Lor and those who had come to kill her, between Lor and the last of the ironclad king's adherents, locking them in my obscene gaze. "She is mine," I growled. "*Mine* to kill. *Mine* to hoard. *Mine* to protect."

As I spoke, a phantom rose behind me in smoky ash-gray magic, peeling itself back from my skin. A dragon, long and lithe, sonorous in its soft, rustling growth. Its serrated spines sliced the sky. Bearded and wingless, its body coiled upward in whirls of blue, white, red, deep green, and stormy black. Sparking silver-white currents roiled through its swirling tail, reaching to join the clouded heavens, while its head and forelegs reared over my shoulders.

"You want her? Come, then."

Behind me, my true form raised its two forepaws, and those who had come to take what belonged to me began to shout—"Dragon! It's a dragon!"—and scatter away. I lifted my hand, curled into a claw, miming my mother before the altar stone. *I* was the lightning. *I* the storm.

"Descend, my wrath! Fulfill my vengeance!"

Lightning broke from the sky, flinging out from the eddy of my tail. Fifty bolts struck fifty fleeing humans and fifty fleeing horses, turning them to dust on the moor. Dust as my kin had been made dust.

It was done at last. The tempestuousness in my being subsided, leaving only quiet embers. The internal fire of a dragon.

When the thunder had rumbled away with my phantom, I turned and knelt, my grin stretching back from sharp teeth.

"By all the gods," Cel'burn murmured. "You truly are a dragon."

I ignored him, addressing myself to Lor.

"I am Quinn, last scion of the dragon. My queen. My lover. My *treasure*. I came seeking revenge for my kin, but that is pointless now. You are not the one who killed them. He is dead. *You killed him*. Now you are mine to protect."

Lor regarded me with her single eye. Her gaze flickered in a recognition I at last took for what it was as I blended it with

Cel'burn's words. Vacuous of me to have not seen it from the first. My queen had known me, even in Dragon Foundry; she had known me and revealed herself to me with intent. She had allowed me my chance for revenge.

"You will serve me, then?" she asked.

My grin tugged wider, knowing it for jest. "I am dragon. *I am free.* I serve no one, not even the gods."

A rising light danced on the queen's face, reflected from the sky, which had been dim for so long. "Then I am to be possessed by you alone? Without equality? Have you forgotten that I, too, am free? But let it be. I am yours. Come, tell me more stories, if you will."

I unfolded to my feet with a growl of pleasure and did so, as the clouds shattered apart and the sun returned to the land. In Dragon Foundry, I had allowed a split stone to flow together and a beacon to reach back to the heavens.

Rebirth

Celosia Crane

The wind whipped around me, stinging my face with tiny snow crystals. Never in the thousands of years of my existence had I been so exposed, so vulnerable. Curling up my body, I wrapped my arms around my protruding belly. A soft gust of warmth rushed against my neck as the stag behind me settled, shifting its bulk.

He was gone. And now I knew I would never see him again. The day after he left me in our mountain home, I had woken with the knowledge that he had gone to his death.

Two weeks had passed since the messenger came bearing the order for him to return home. Two weeks I had held that knowledge and now the knowledge that my time was approaching. I was running out of time.

I pictured him in my mind: Birger, my human husband. Broad shoulders and long blond hair. His gentle eyes had reflected the sky, just like my favorite mountain pools. He had come to the mountains to hunt many, many months ago. Instead, he had found me.

Now I was left with our children growing within this fragile human body. Squeezing my eyes shut, I tried to fight the grief that was building in my chest. The pressure expanded until a cry erupted from my lips. Everything in this frail human body hurt.

I longed to feel the wind beneath my wings again, the freedom of dancing on the air currents. But that was impossible for the time being.

Within my belly, the babes moved restlessly. Cold and stiff, I pulled the cloak more tightly around my body. Turning my head, I buried my face in the stag's shoulder. Exhaustion slowly took over, and I slipped into an uneasy sleep.

I slept badly. The ground was hard, and the babes were restless. Early morning found me struggling to my feet, picking up the long yew staff I had found the day before, and pressing forward.

I had to make it down the mountain. I had to find Birger's people in one of the human villages along the coast. It was almost time.

The stag remained with me for a good portion of that day. His stately antlers bobbed above his long nose and large, liquid eyes. I leaned gratefully against his shoulder, welcoming both the warmth and support. My hips hurt, and each step caused pain to shoot up my back.

We reached the tree line in the middle of the afternoon. My white stag snorted softly before he tossed his head and turned back around, disappearing into the forest.

Standing in the last shadows of the pines, I breathed in their slightly acrid and pungent scent as I stared out over the rolling foothills. In the distance, I could see the smoke rising from a settlement or farm. I only hoped there was enough daylight left to reach it.

Settling my fur cape more securely across my shoulders, I pushed my white-blonde hair back from my face. Then I breathed deeply and set out in the direction of the smoke. A swift kick from one of the babes had me grunting as it nearly knocked me to my knees.

"Now, girls." My hand rubbed gently over the spot. "Be kind to your mother."

It was almost fully dark when I reached the farmstead. I could smell the animals in the barn. The sod house that stood in the center of the small complex exuded warmth and comfort. As I walked into the center courtyard, a man exited the house and began making his way across the open land toward the barn.

When he spotted me, he froze for a moment, then hurried toward me. "What are you doing out so late, lady? It's dangerous! There's a large wolf pack in the area."

As he approached me, he slowed down, and the genuine concern on his face suddenly shifted. His gaze became shuttered, and his steps slowed further. "I've never seen anyone who looks like you before. Who are you?"

I took a small step forward, watching him carefully. Some people considered me an enemy, and while I might have been immortal, this human body was very fragile.

"My name is Aash. I have been journeying for several days." One of the babes kicked me hard again, and my hand flew to my belly. "Please, I am looking for somewhere to sleep. And maybe a little something to eat?"

His eyes widened yet again as his gaze dropped to where my hand lay protectively against my stomach. I watched the color drain from his face before he turned and started walking back toward the house.

"You can sleep in the barn tonight. I'll see if the missus will spare any food for you." His tone was incredulous, and he shook his head as he glanced back over his shoulder to look at me, as though he could not believe I was really there. "Wait here. I'll be back."

A few long moments passed, and an argument rose within the house. Then a woman wrapped in a thick wool shawl emerged from the house, clutching a bowl between her hands. "Come on, already. The soup will be cold." Her voice was hard, and she proffered the bowl grudgingly.

I took it from her, feeling the warmth radiate slowly through my hands. Lifting the crude spoon, I chewed and swallowed the thick stew. Warmth slid down my throat, carrying with it nutrients I had been lacking these past few days as I made my way down the mountain toward the villages.

"Where are you headed that you are traveling at your advanced stage?" I could feel the burning curiosity in the woman, but there was also disapproval and a hint of fear.

"I seek my husband's people."

That was the truth. I would not be able to raise our children once they were born. They needed humans. I was one in shape only. Once they were born, I would revert to my true shape.

"Where is your husband?" Her voice had thickened with suspicion, but I was too busy eating to watch her expression.

When I'd finished, I handed back the empty bowl. "Thank you. I feel much warmer already." Resting a hand on my stomach, I closed my eyes. "My husband has gone to fight with the men of his home." I swallowed hard. "He received orders from his chieftain two weeks ago."

The woman harrumphed and took the shawl off her shoulders. Handing it to me, she almost growled, "Here, take this. It will help to keep you warm."

I took the soft woolen garment, letting my fingers sink into it before I wrapped it around my shoulders. "Thank you. I shall not forget your kindness."

Her husband returned, a bundle of blankets in his arms. "Come on. I'll show you the hay mow."

Turning away from the woman, I followed her husband into the long, low building that sat directly opposite the house. Cattle lowed in the darkness, and a few nervous bleats sounded from the sheep and goats that were penned within.

Walking past the animals, the farmer led me to a large pile of fragrant hay. He thrust the blankets into my arms, his voice gruff. "The wife insists you leave tomorrow morning."

I nodded. "Thank her for me, please. I must leave either way. I still have a long way to go, and my time is running out."

"There is a village a day's walk from here. I hope, for your sake, that you find your husband's people there."

I nodded again. "Me as well."

He stood awkwardly in the darkness. "Do you know the name of the village your husband comes from?"

I shook my head slowly. "No, but I will know those of his bloodline."

In the light from the house, I could see his body stiffen. "I'm afraid to ask how you'll know."

I smiled. "You remarked on my appearance when you first saw me. As well you might, for there is no one who looks like me."

He turned but paused in the doorway looking back over his shoulder. "Who are you?"

I smiled gently. "I am Aashutosh, the great dragon. Though I have held this human form for little over a year."

He stood frozen in the doorway for a long moment before shaking his head in disbelief. "Good night, lady."

When he was gone, I took in a deep breath, easing the tension that ran through my shoulders. I had survived this first encounter. And I even received a somewhat warm welcome.

Glancing around at the animals, I smiled and spoke a blessing on the farm. "For your kindness to one who was a stranger, I grant you prosperity and my protection. Your cows and ewes will be fertile, the land shall bless you, and the wolves will keep away."

Unfolding the first blanket the farmer had given me, I laid it down on the sweet dried grass. Curling up, I wrapped the other blanket around my shoulders and closed my eyes, falling into the deepest sleep I had experienced in the last few months.

I awoke to the bleating of sheep and the lowing of cattle. Relieving my bladder in an empty stall, I quickly shook my deerskin dress back into place and gathered up my staff and the shawl. Though it had been given grudgingly, I had felt the honesty behind the gift. The woman had given it truly.

As I reached the edge of the farmstead, a small girl ran after me. She held a basket out to me. "Please, take this with you!"

Crouching down, I smiled and accepted the basket. "And what is this, little one?"

She smiled, ignoring the calls for her to come back to the house. "It's a loaf of bread. I baked it myself! And there's some cheese and a few winter apples." She twisted her hands in her skirt. "I didn't have much else."

I placed my hand gently on her head. "Thank you, child."

She looked up at me, her face suffused with delight. "My name is Narah."

I smiled back, accepting the basket. "Thank you, Narah. My name is Aashutosh."

Narah's eyes went wide. "Are you really a dragon? Mama didn't believe Papa when he told her who you were."

I chuckled. "Yes, though right now, I am human, like you." Pressing a kiss to her forehead, I levered myself back to my feet with my staff. "Your gift is a great boon, Narah. I shall never forget your kindness." She grinned and threw her arms around me in an awkward hug, then turned and ran back to the house.

My connection with Birger was growing weaker, and I knew he was not long for this world. It was his spirit that had drawn me on so far. The knowledge that I would know his people because of our connection had been what kept me going all these long days.

Now it had faded to a mere shadow. For the first time in my immortal existence, I felt my heart cracking.

Ahead of me, though still a few miles off, lay another village. Beyond it, I could see the steel gray of the sea spread out to the horizon.

The pain in my lower back was getting stronger, coming in

waves as it shot up my spine and down my legs. I had to make it there before the babes decided it was time.

Gripping my staff more tightly, I forced my feet to move at a brisk pace. I had to get there.

I had to.

Pain radiated through my body as I entered the village. Gasping loudly, I stumbled against the nearest house. Around me, people bustled about their business. In the harbor, tall ships were being repaired and made ready.

So far, no one had noticed a lone woman, a stranger, in the beginning stages of labor. I pressed forward, clinging to my staff tightly as another sharp wave of pain rippled across my belly and sank its teeth deeply into my back. Unable to stop myself, I cried out loudly and fell to my hands and knees, the staff forgotten.

Several women surrounded me. "Come on, Astrid. Help me get her to her feet. Mother will be able to help her." Hands gently gripped my arms as I was lifted to my feet.

They half carried me across the village square and into a longhouse on the far side. I opened my eyes when the light changed, growing darker.

"Mother!" the first young woman cried loudly into the emptiness of the longhouse.

"Ingrid, what is the fuss about?" A tall woman stood from the fireside and walked toward us.

"She's gone into labor, Mother."

I felt, rather than saw, what happened next. The woman they called Mother stepped forward, her rough hand resting for a moment upon my belly. Then she spoke in a sharp commanding tone. "Take her to my room. Then, Astrid, I want you to get some water boiling."

Again, the two young women half carried me across the room and into another chamber, where they laid me on a bed. Mother came up beside me and crouched next to the bed. Her voice was calm and firm.

"I am Solveig Algar. I have helped bring many of the babes in this town into the world. Do not fear."

Her voice rose slightly as she issued orders. "Ingrid, bring me more firewood and several more blankets."

As her hand drifted gently over my belly, feeling for contractions, I felt it. It was there. The ghostly connection I still had with Birger flamed as I laid my hand over hers. I had found them.

Panting, I raised myself on my elbows and stared at her. She turned her head, and I saw the same sky in her eyes and the same warmth in her face.

Tears rose, and this time I did not fight them. Nor the relief that accompanied them.

"What is it, child?" Her voice was as soft as the hand on my belly.

"I found you." My voice caught in my throat. "You are Birger's people."

Shock widened her eyes as she drew in a sharp breath. "How do you know my son?"

Before I could answer, another wave of pain tore through me. Unable to help myself, I screamed. Her hand on my belly went stiff, and she nodded. "It's almost time."

For a while, it was silent in the room except for my labored breathing and cries of pain. Solveig worked calmly as I sobbed and panted through each set of contractions.

When there was a lull, she lifted a ceramic cup to my lips. "Drink. Then tell me how you know my son."

I swallowed the cool liquid, tasting the sweetness of honey. Then I met her eyes. "I carry his children." My voice was soft and gentle.

She nodded as tears gathered in her eyes. Leaning forward, she pressed a kiss to my forehead. "I am glad you made it," she whispered. "He was a haunted man when he disappeared into the mountains. I thought for sure I had lost my son forever." She brushed the hair back from my forehead. "Then he returned three weeks ago." She smiled. "He spoke of you. His beautiful Aash."

She paused suddenly, looking at me again. "Children?"

I nodded, watching as the tears spilled from her eyes. She shook her head sadly. "If only . . ."

I took her hand. "I know. I knew the day after he left me." I saw comprehension in her eyes, shock and pain, but even more, surprise. Before she could speak, another wave of contractions swept through me.

After that, we did not speak. The pain came closer and closer together. Soon, a tiny wail filled the room. Solveig handed the babe to Astrid and turned back to me. "She's a fine, beautiful girl child."

But it was not over yet. I smiled, feeling only the need to finish this task. Once it was over, I could return to my true shape. Then I could return home to my mountains, where I could properly mourn Birger. My handsome warrior.

I pushed, working with this human body as a second cry joined the first. A few minutes passed before a third, and then a fourth, joined in. With the birth of the fourth child, the sharp, strong pain of the contractions ceased, leaving a low throbbing pain in its wake. That was easily borne.

Solveig and Ingrid laid the babes down beside me. I looked at their tiny red faces and even tinier clawed fingers. My daughters were beautiful.

Solveig made me comfortable before pulling a chair up beside me. Her face, while wreathed in awe, was also full of sadness. She gripped my hand tightly. "My child." She swallowed hard. "I must tell you."

I squeezed her hand in return. "I already know, Solveig." I continued speaking before she could. "Birger and I shared a special bond. I could feel his presence, even when he was not with me." I closed my eyes as tears trickled down my cheeks. "I knew the day after he left me that he was going to his death. That this war would take him from me."

I opened my eyes and turned to her. "I never told him just how close I was."

Solveig nodded. "He would not have left you if you had. Not my Birger."

I smiled. "No, he would not have. And when he left, I expected him to return, so I did not feel the need to accompany him. I was happy in my home in the mountains."

I closed my eyes again, feeling the four tiny bodies that surrounded me. "I loved him, as I have never loved before. For him, and for this world, I gave birth to these children. They are my gift to you all."

I swallowed hard; the exhaustion of everything was taking over. Solveig laid her hand gently against my forehead before standing up. "Sleep now, Aash. Astrid, Ingrid, and I shall keep watch. There is nothing here that can harm you."

With her words, sleep overtook me.

While my skin was still incredibly pale and my hair almost silver in the sunlight, my clothing was now warm and colorful, decorated with intricate embroidery like the rest of the family's.

On the twelfth day after the birth of my daughters, I stood on the pier, leaning on my yew staff and staring out at the dark sea. Birger's father, Grim Algar, had told me the remainder of the story. How their ship had been ambushed during the night as they sailed toward their enemies.

It had sunk, and few had survived, clinging to the wreckage. Now, as I stared out at the horizon, I could not shake the fear that had settled into my bones.

Something was coming. It brought danger and evil. Like the coming of winter, I could scent it on the winds.

Their enemies were approaching, and my new family was in danger.

I walked swiftly back to the Algar longhouse. Upon entering, I watched as Solveig rocked one of the little ones in her arms. Looking up, she met my gaze. "Is something wrong, Aash?"

Walking across the room, I held out my arms to take my daughter and cradle her close against my chest. Her eyelids fluttered and her breath evened out as she sank into sleep.

Lifting my head, I met Solveig's gaze. "They are coming here."

As her gaze held mine, her jaw clenched and she straightened her shoulders. "I shall go get Grim."

I nodded and sank down into a chair near the fire. From the other room, a small pipping cry rose on the air. Rising, I walked into the room and laid the sleeping babe down upon the soft furs of the bed; then I lifted her sister into my arms.

"Hush, little one. Now is not the time for cries." She settled swiftly in my arms. Staring down at her, I knew. My time with them was drawing to a close.

I smiled down at her. "I must give you all names." My chest tightened as I cuddled the little one close. "You all deserve strong, powerful names, for you are going to bring much change into this world."

Behind me, I could feel Ingrid's and Astrid's presence as they entered the room quietly. Lying swaddled upon the bed, my children opened their eyes. Leaning over, I laid the babe I held beside her sisters.

"My children, you are more than human. Your father was human, yes. But your mother is a dragon." Behind me, I heard Astrid and Ingrid draw in sharp breaths. "I loved your father, and I love you. But I cannot stay with you."

I reached out and brushed a cheek with one hand. "It breaks my heart. But you are safe with your father's family. I will name you now."

Behind me, Astrid and Ingrid drew closer.

I touched the babe closest to me on the head, feeling her downy hair. "You will be Jord, for the earth. You will grow strong and call upon animals and plants to do your bidding."

My hand moved to the next head. "Luft, you shall call upon the winds and all the weather and birds that fly."

My fingers brushed across the next babe's cheek. "Brand, my little darling. You shall be filled with spirit and call upon fire, in all its forms. Thermal hot springs and volcanoes alike will answer your call."

My hand danced across the hair of the final child. "And Vatten. You, my little one, will love the water above all else. You shall speak to the water creatures and swim like the otters. Even in the cold of winter, you shall help your family find fish beneath the thick sea ice."

Footsteps in the hall made me turn, and I met Grim's solemn face. Blinking back tears, I turned and dropped kisses to each babe's face.

Grim nodded as I turned back around. "Aye, lass. They are coming." He cocked his head. "How did you know?"

I grinned, and for the first time since the birth, I felt my skin begin to shift. Grim must have seen something of it in my face, for he took a step backward and dropped to his knees. "Aashutosh, I did not recognize you. Forgive me." I could hear the wonder of the name on his tongue.

Stretching out one hand, I touched his shoulder. "We do not have time for that, Grim Algar. Birger knew the truth and loved me as I am. Now, I will help protect your village and people. The Algars will always have my protection."

I glanced back at my children, then met Astrid's and Ingrid's gazes. "I will not be able to stay, after this."

Grim nodded, his expression sorrowful. "Do not fear. We shall take good care of them."

"I know."

Turning, I led the way out into the great room. Gathered there were all the remaining men and lads who were old enough to carry a sword and shield. Grim took his seat, even as the men all stared at me in astonishment.

"We have been alerted. The Gunnarsens are approaching. They think to catch us off guard."

He indicated me. "Little do they know who exactly we have fighting alongside us."

The men murmured as they turned to stare at me. Straightening my shoulders, I focused on the energy that had been building within me since I had given birth. I felt my skin shifting just enough for these men to see that I was not human.

Stepping toward the fire, I spoke, power pouring through my voice. "I am Aashutosh. Having borne a human shape for the last twelve months, I am now free to resume my natural form, to defend your city. Birger Algar was my husband. I fight alongside you."

We had little time for further talk. The warning bell down at the harbor began to clang, its hollow tones echoing through the hall. The men rushed from the room, while all the women came in through the back door.

Turning to Grim, I smiled, making sure to show my teeth as they stretched into their natural elongated forms. "Go and fight. Do not worry about the women and children. I shall protect them."

He nodded, his eyes still wide with awe. Then he was gone. Turning, I met Solveig's gaze, mine flicking to the sword she carried. "Keep them safe for me." I saw her nod before I turned and walked out of the longhouse.

Behind me, I heard Astrid and Ingrid cry out, but I did not listen. This was my task now. This was my family.

The energy within me was like fire in my veins, calling me back to my natural form. Closing my eyes, I focused. My bones shifted— stretching, growing. The pain was bad, but not as bad as labor had been.

I gritted my teeth as my nose and jaw extended. My arms lengthened, and wings sprouted from my back. My torso stretched, rib cage expanding and changing shape as my skin shifted, scales taking the place of tender flesh.

Then it was done. My long, sinewy body had returned.

I stretched my wings experimentally and rose on my hind legs. My foreclaws pawed at the air as I flapped, screaming in defiance. I could hear the battle as my husband's people engaged their enemies along the wharf: men crying out, swords clashing, wood splintering. Flapping my wings, I rose slowly over the Algar's longhouse.

I was just clearing the longhouse roof when, above the noise, I heard it.

"Aashutosh!"

It was a voice I knew. A voice I had never thought to hear again.

Turning my head, I saw a ship holding back at a distance from the harbor. Flying closer, I spied a man tied to its mast.

I knew. Gaunt and hollow eyed, Birger stared up at me. Beside him stood a large warrior, one hand buried in Birger's hair, the other holding a knife to his throat. With a laugh, the warrior drew the blade sharply across Birger's throat.

I could hear Grim's scream of fury and pain echo from the quay. I knew that by forcing Birger's people to watch his death, the Gunnarsens had hoped to weaken their opponents or, at the very least, taunt them with their power.

A scream burst out of my chest as my body spiraled higher and higher into the air. Heat grew in the back of my throat as I swept down toward the harbor. Birger's body hung limp against the mast now, taunting me. Mocking me with its lifelessness.

I swept down and fire erupted from my mouth as I screamed out my pain and fury. One clawed foot reached out and snatched up my love's murderer in a tight grip. He screamed and thrashed as my talons pierced his body. High in the air, far above the harbor, I released him. I watched him plummet, strike the water, and disappear.

There would be no mercy.

The smoke was dissipating when I once again settled upon my four legs before the Algar's longhouse. Momentary flashes of pain swept through me until I was once again standing on two human legs.

Solveig rushed forward with a blanket to cover my naked body, then led me in to where my daughters lay asleep.

"They are safe, Aashutosh." She stood a little farther back than she would have before, as though she were afraid.

I smiled sadly. "Solveig, I am still Aash to you and your family. I have given the babes their names. They will all bear unique gifts of power as they grow. Gifts that will tie them to this world and bring about a great change. They are my gift to this world."

"What now?" Solveig's voice trembled slightly as she turned her gaze back to the sleeping babies.

"I must leave." I turned and faced Solveig. "Take care of them for me, please." Leaning down, I brushed kisses across their foreheads.

"I shall return every spring"—I looked up as tears filled my eyes—"to be with them for a short period of time, to teach them and love them. But I must not stay too long."

Solveig, Astrid, and Ingrid all nodded. Solveig spoke quietly but firmly. "We will watch over them, I promise."

Astrid and Ingrid were crying quietly behind their mother. I reached out a hand to each of them. "I can never thank you enough for your quick thinking and actions to bring me here when I most needed it." I squeezed their hands. "Watch over my little girls."

Turning, I walked back out into the great room. There, Grim and his men had recovered Birger's body from the scorched mast and laid it on a bench. His limp body bore the marks of my fire, and tonight, my beloved's body would blaze as he was properly mourned. As it should be.

Walking over, I knelt beside his body and brushed my lips across the now-cool forehead. Then I nodded to Grim. "I shall return."

He nodded. "We will be here."

Walking back outside, I dropped the blanket and shifted. A long, sinewy body, covered in scales, talons, and sharp teeth, replaced my human exterior. With a running leap, I flapped my wings and lifted up into the sky.

Circling above the house, I looked down for a moment before turning resolutely and winging my way to the north.

I would return each spring to be with the gifts that Birger had given me. Our children would awaken a new age. Through them, magic would return to the land.

fire legacy

Hayley Green

My husband, Matthew, came home after receiving his job assignment in the village. He looked stricken.

We had never been close. Why would we be when I had broken all the village's expectations of women on a daily basis? Matthew had wanted a wife who was obedient and did as she was told, quietly and without complaint—like we were supposed to. I was none of those things.

"What's wrong?" I asked as soon I saw the look on his face. "Don't tell me you got sanitation. I don't need to smell that all day, every day. Cleaning out our own bucket is enough."

He frowned at me and crossed his arms. "That's not funny, Phoenix."

I gave a wry smile. "Really? I thought it was brilliant."

He gave a frustrated groan and muttered under his breath. I only caught bits and pieces.

"Don't tell me you're going the way of the crazies. I'm not prepared to deal with that commitment this young. Not that I really have a choice in the matter now."

He looked at me blankly. "That's just the problem, Phoenix. I got stuck with a razor-tongued outcast for a wife, and I don't get a say in the matter. You disappear for hours on end without telling anyone where you're going. On top of that, they assigned me to a very hard job. I can't fathom why they would want me for it."

I gasped and pointed at him. "You did get assigned to sanitation. I *knew* it!"

He shook his head and walked to the bedroom, not even turning around to say his parting words. "I'm going to bed. Stay on the couch tonight."

I balled up my fists and glared at the old couch, which smelled of mildew. No way was I sleeping on that. I would go see Agni instead. He had a bed in his lair, and I was welcome to it anytime. I grabbed my cloak, pulled the black hood over my head, and pulled the sides close around me. Keeping my head bent, I walked through the village, making my way out the secret entrance the Protectors used to get in and out of town. It was a direct path to Agni's lair.

I walked through the rough scrub of the forest, feeling the cloak catch on brambles and thorns. The forest wasn't kind to travelers. That was why Agni preferred to have the inhospitable forest surround his mountain: for protection. The ground inclined steeply after an hour, and the undergrowth grew thicker. In the dark, it was a lot harder to see where I was placing my feet. I stumbled over loose stones and roots, landing on my hands and knees and getting thorns and thistles lodged in my hands. They stung, but Agni kept bandages and cleaning agents for that reason.

When I was a kid, I'd only been able to visit Agni when both of my parents were asleep. I would have had to be back before dawn, with all the thorns, brambles, and specks of dirt cleaned from my cloak. Since I escaped my parents' house, my visits with Agni were longer, and I'd grown lax in cleaning my cloak. Matthew wasn't thrilled with my nighttime strolls or the bandages that appeared on my hands in the morning.

The thicket cleared, revealing ground blackened with soot that had escaped through the hole in the top of the mountain and settled over the land. Agni breathed out soot like an old smoker hacked up tar. It was a consequence of what he was. Every breath released tendrils of smoke, and black dust covered everything in his lair—except for the riches he obsessively polished every day.

I found the cave and moved the heavy rock just enough for me to slip around it. Being small and strong had its advantages. The cave was dark and sloped downhill at a sharp angle, and there were lots of twists, turns, and false ends. Agni didn't want to be found.

When I got to the entrance of his lair, two torches illuminated my face, and Agni's great yellow catlike eye was staring through the bars, taking up the whole window in the door.

"I thought it might be you, Phoenix. Another nighttime visit? I take it the marriage isn't going so well, then." The door swung open. The dragon moved away from the door, revealing a large cavern the size of the Elders' town hall. Agni curled up in the corner, but he still took up a significant part of the room, about a third. He left the feather bed he had gotten for me open. The white sheets were gray with years of soot. I closed and locked the door behind me, then took a running leap onto the bed.

I coughed a little as a cloud of black dust puffed up in the air as I landed. "Oh, Agni. You've no idea. He's upset over whatever job he got. He relegated me to the couch again for the night. We haven't slept in the same bed since our wedding night. You should have seen his face when he saw it was me they had matched him with. He looked so disgusted and disappointed. They wanted him to be a 'good influence' on me. It's the first time he's ever failed at something."

Two great claws hovered nearby, holding a sturdy wooden box pinched between them. I took the box from Agni and cleaned the wounds on my hands, hissing at the sting.

"I know. You've already told me many more times than I can count."

"How old are you?" I asked offhandedly.

His eye regarded me from the level of my head. "Tens of thousands of years. I stopped counting the individual years. I count by centuries now." His eye blinked. It had taken me a while to get used to the reptilian way he blinked.

"Exactly. You can count a lot higher than the number of times I've told you that story. Besides, it's only been two days since it happened. I can't possibly have told you that story tens of thousands of times in the single visit I've had with you since the event."

A toothy grin and puffs of smoke appeared as he laughed. "You'd be surprised how many ways you told me in the first ten minutes of your visit."

I threw a pillow at him, but he caught it and feathers exploded everywhere as it popped between his claws.

"You're in a mood," he said, eyeing me.

I flopped down on my back and stared up at the stars I could see through the hollow top of the mountain. "I don't see this marriage working out."

"Don't give up, child." A giant paw gently turned my face toward Agni, careful not to touch the razor-sharp ends of his claws to me or the bed. "Don't avoid his eyes. Stand up for yourself. You are not submissive. You have a fire in you. Never forget that."

I rolled my eyes. "So you keep saying."

He laughed, and the booming sound shook the walls of the cavern. Some rocks came loose and pinged off the gold covering the floor. "This is what I like about you. You're so refreshing to talk to. You aren't afraid of me. Most Protectors treat me like I'm some angry god they must fear or get struck down by my fury."

"You? Scary? Pfft. You're as gentle as a kitten."

"Don't make me burn you to a crisp. I may like you, but calling me a kitten is a crime punishable by death."

I put my hands up in a surrendering pose. "Don't burn me to a crisp yet. I'd taste much better with a side of my secret sauce."

He barked out laughter again. "You must triple the portions for a meal your size."

"Triple? More like a hundredfold. I'm bigger than a brisket. Although I'm not sure how tasty my lungs would be, filled with soot as they are. Spending time with you has made me cough up tar on more than one occasion."

Agni smiled a toothy grin. It would have terrified any who didn't know him. "Have you been practicing with your fire?"

In answer, I lifted one finger, focused my mind, and concentrated my eyes on my pointer finger, getting the fire to flow from my fingertip. I wrote *Yes* backward so he could read it, the word hovering in the air, made of fiery letters.

He nodded. "You are mastering the art. Many of your townspeople could not have brought forth fire from a single finger."

"Well, there's not much else to do once I finish chores. I mean, I could read the ancient book, but you've already told me most of it."

Agni smiled again. "You never were one for idleness." He paused and blew a smoke ring into the air. "You need sleep, Phoenix. I have arranged a surprise for you in the village. You'll receive it tomorrow." He blew out the torches, so the only light in the cave came from the stars and his glowing eyes, which he closed, throwing the lair into darkness.

"A surprise?" I asked the darkness.

"Shush, child. Patience is more becoming of you. Besides, anticipation is better than the gift."

"I don't know if I agree with that statement."

"Well, you won't be getting any answers from me," he said, his eyes still closed.

"You're a killjoy." I crossed my arms and lay down, staring up at the night sky.

"Would you expect anything less?"

I had to smile at that. "No."

"Then that's settled. Go to sleep."

I closed my eyes too and relaxed into the soft mattress and remaining pillow.

I opened my eyes to voices. Agni had visitors. It was probably the Protectors. There would be a new one being trained, what with all the eighteen-year-old males being assigned their places in the village. They expected women to be homemakers and have children.

I sat up and let out a silent breath of relief when I saw Agni had positioned himself between me and the door. No one knew where I ran off to at night, and Agni liked to keep it that way.

"What is your name, new one?" Agni asked.

The answering voice surprised me. "Matthew," my husband said. My resulting gasp echoed around the cavern. It was followed by silence, except for the sound of my hand slapping over my mouth.

"Agni," Elder John spoke sternly. "I thought we agreed you would quit snacking on the young maidens a long time ago."

"Her? She's not a snack. She's a friend of mine. Although she has promised me a secret sauce to go along with her once I finally do barbecue her."

"Secret . . . secret sauce?" Matthew said. Shit. He was putting two and two together.

"Let us pass, Agni," Elder John said, his voice rough from years of breathing the smoky air in Agni's cave. I would probably sound like that in a couple of years, myself.

"I don't think that's a good idea."

"It's Phoenix, isn't it?" Matthew said, his voice flat. "That's why the council wants to see her. Why she comes home from being out all night with dirt, soot, and brambles all over her cloak. She's been coming to see you."

Agni was silent. The eye facing me blinked slowly, and I knew the other one would be too. He was weighing his words.

"I would not punish her. She is under my protection. I stripped the Protector status of the last person to punish her for seeing me, had his power of fire taken away, and branded him with the curse of the dragon. He has been out of work for a long time. No one wants a person cursed by a dragon to work for them."

I could practically see the scowl on Matthew's face. Agni lifted his head, and I slipped off the bed, still fully clothed, and passed the stoic Elder John and an angry Matthew, who was dressed in the standard Protector robes. "I'll see you at home," I told Matthew. "Some surprise, Agni!" I called back once I was past the two men.

Agni's reply shook the rock. "Well, I had to meet your husband somehow, Phoenix."

Back in town, an Elder accosted me on the main road as I made my way back home. "Phoenix, they have requested you as a Protector." He handed me robes black as night with red satin trim. The robes of the Protectors. "Change. Agni said you already know him, so that's taken care of. Elder John will update you on the state of things. He should come down the mountain in a few hours."

"A Protector?" I asked. But the Elder was already walking away. This must have been Agni's real surprise. Sneaky dragon. I shook my head, a smile on my face as I walked home to change.

Matthew walked in sometime later, his mouth set in a grim line. "Why didn't you tell me?"

I shrugged. "Don't take it personally. No one else knows about it, other than Oscar."

"Oscar?" He sounded like he was close to erupting in anger. He crossed his arms over his chest, his eyes tracking me the way they would a deer he was hunting.

"My father, if you could call him that. He went against Agni and forbade me from seeing him. It didn't work out well for him when the old dragon found out."

Matthew made a disgusted sound. "A female Protector. Ridiculous."

Elder John entered our house in time to hear Matthew's comment. "Be careful what you say, Matthew. Phoenix is under Agni's protection. It doesn't matter that you are her husband; if you threaten her, you will end up like Oscar.

"Which brings me to the news at hand. Other settlements of Pyros are being attacked and destroyed. Someone who knows how to disable the dragons' ability to use fire is slaughtering them and the villages who protect them. Someone with the dragon's curse from Agni himself."

"Oscar," I whispered. I wasn't surprised by how low he had fallen. I balled up my fists as memories flooded my mind. How he would hurt my mother and me. How relieved I'd felt when he left.

Elder John nodded. "That's why your job has become more important than ever. Only those most skilled in the arts of fire may become Protectors now. You will protect not only the dragon but the village. If all the dragons die, summer dies with them, as described in the ancient book. Don't fail us now." He fixed us with a piercing stare until we nodded. "You start tomorrow." Then he left.

Matthew faced me, took a breath as if he were about to say something, paused, seemed to think better of it, and disappeared into the bedroom. I knew not to follow.

Ten months later, I was feeling restless. My stomach had grown with new life. The Elders and Matthew had forbidden me from performing my duties as Protector, and I hadn't seen Agni in five months. Having a one-month-old, however, did not slow me down in the least.

The midwife had named my daughter Pele. She was healthy and strong.

Matthew had become colder than usual with me, remarking in frustration that Agni kept asking about the baby and me. The dragon kept threatening him too. Agni thought Matthew was trying to keep me from seeing him. No matter how many letters I sent Agni, Matthew was still threatened nearly every day. He was not happy about it.

However badly he treated me, though, Matthew was a wonderful father. Pele had him wrapped around her little finger.

One month after Pele's birth, Matthew was up at the crack of dawn to go check on Agni. I, however, was up before him, wearing my Protector robes and a tight sling that secured Pele within my cloak to protect her from the thorns.

Matthew took one look at me and sighed. "I suppose there is

nothing I can do to stop you from joining me, is there?" I shook my head, smiling eagerly. He would let me go without a fight. "Just keep Pele away from the thorns."

He never looked back as we climbed our way up the mountain. When we reached Agni's lair, the dragon was looking out the window, as always. He swung open the door with a flourish when he saw me, his fangs showing with his smile. It looked a lot like when he bared his teeth in a snarl. Matthew flinched.

"Let me see this child of yours, Phoenix. You've no idea how boring your husband is with conversation."

I couldn't help but let out an unseemly snort of laughter. Matthew glared at me, and I shrugged. Matthew stayed at the doorway while I pushed past him into the lair and sat on the bed, unwrapping Pele. The dragon took one look at the baby and said, "She has your hair and his eyes. What a striking combination."

I nodded. "I'm told the green eyes and auburn hair are signs of strength for the gift of fire."

"Don't listen to those old legends. It's more about the practice. Have you written her the letter?"

I nodded and pulled the letter from my cloak, the cream envelope lush against my fingers. She would receive the letter on her eighteenth birthday, activating her powers with the spelled ink we had used, blessed by Agni himself. The letter was tradition amongst the Pyros.

The door suddenly slammed closed and Matthew locked it, startling us. I folded the letter back into its rightful pocket. Agni quieted, and we could hear fast footfalls easily navigating the path to the dragon's lair, without hesitation. Agni let out a low growl that shook the walls. The footsteps didn't falter.

"Get behind me, Matthew. Protect your wife and daughter if I fail."

My heart beat faster. My voice shook. "Agni, you weren't expecting a visit from the Elders today, were you?"

He shook his head and brought a claw to his mouth in a silent gesture for me to not talk. He put his eye next to the window. The lair was silent as we waited. The air was tense, and every muscle was tight, ready to spring into action.

The footsteps slowed, and Agni screeched in pain. His head snapped away from the window, displaying a gaping hole where his eye had been. Purple blood streamed down his face, and my stomach roiled. A sword hacked away at the door.

Matthew pointed to the secret exit that had recently been built, but I shook my head. I kept my eyes focused on the window, where I could see the face of the dragon slayer. It was Oscar, my estranged and disgraced father.

My blood boiled. He would not hurt Agni anymore. I concentrated on his face as he burst through the door, building the fire with my mind. He screamed in pain as the fire I started burned his face beyond repair. He thrashed about with his sword, coming closer with every slash to Agni, who couldn't see him.

Despite the fire blinding him, Oscar still had impeccable aim. He stabbed Agni in the throat. Agni's fiery breath whimpered out in a spark of purple blood and black tar. Agni could no longer use his fire. I screamed, ignoring Matthew's shouts to stay back as he focused his fire on roasting Oscar alive.

I reached Agni, tears streaming down my face. His strained voice muttered a spell in the dragon tongue. He had taught me enough to know what he was doing. He was cursing the gold. No one could use it except for . . . Pele?

My vision blurred. "Agni, I can't lose you. You'll be fine. Everything has to be fine." Even as I spoke the words, I knew they weren't true. If I repeated them, maybe they would become true. Agni was still breathing, after all.

I sucked in a shaky breath. He was alive. That was all that mattered. I took off my cloak. I had to stem the blood gushing from his throat. It was the only way he would live. I pressed the cloak to the wound with shaky hands.

"Agni, hold this, please." My voice broke. "You're going to be okay."

Agni gave a small smile. "You're the best friend a dragon could ask for." He raised a claw and pressed my cloak against his wound.

"This is not goodbye," I said.

I heard a scream behind me. My father's sword had been run through Matthew's stomach. Oscar was on the ground, badly burned, but he still reached for the weapon. I didn't have time to cry over Agni. I needed that sword. My eyes were useless, blurred by tears, so I wouldn't be able to maintain a fire. But I had one other option.

Holding Pele to my chest, I ran over and grabbed Matthew's sword. I couldn't let Oscar live. He had killed the father of my child. He had hurt Agni. He had beat my mother. He wanted to kill all the dragons. I would not let him go unpunished. I held the sword to Oscar's throat, and he stopped moving.

"Phoenix . . . don't. Get Pele out," Matthew gasped out from behind me. His words sounded wet, as if blood were filling his lungs.

I didn't take my eyes off Oscar. If I had, I would have ended up dead like the rest of them. "Sorry, Matthew. But I must do what's right. And what's right is killing this piece of scum. I will keep Pele safe."

Matthew's labored breaths slowed. I knew they would stop soon. He coughed, trying to get out an answer. But nothing came, and the sound of his breathing stopped.

Agni continued to cough and splutter. I had to finish Oscar quickly so I could help him.

Oscar gave me a weak smile. "Phoenix. My, how you've grown." There was fear in his eyes.

"Don't, Oscar."

"Am I not your father?"

I pressed the sword harder against his throat, drawing a light line of blood, not too deep but enough to make him lean back. "You weren't deserving of that title when you first spilled dragon's blood. Agni has been more of a father than you will ever be."

"I know you're angry, but . . ." His eyes took in my appearance. "You're a Protector? I'm a grandpa?"

"You will never see the light of day again, much less live to see my baby grow. And yes, I'm a Protector."

"Then I suggest you leave soon. The king's men are burning the village as we speak. They are coming to collect the gold."

"Why should I trust you?"

He swallowed. "You have no reason to. Call it regret or the joy of family. Call it whatever you want."

I raised my sword, ready to drive it through his heart, but Agni's claw beat me to it. Oscar was dead. I closed my eyes, relief flooding through me. He would never hurt another soul.

I rushed over to Agni, petting his head in a soothing manner. My cloak had done nothing to stop the blood. It felt as though there wasn't enough air in the cavern. I couldn't breathe. Agni was going to die. I fell to my knees, spreading my arms around his neck. "No, Agni."

"Go, Phoenix. Save Pele. You don't have long." His voice was thick and weak.

"Agni, you can't die." Tears clouded my voice, and Pele began to cry.

"There is no hope left for me. I will do what I can to keep you safe, but you are running out of time. Go."

I hugged him harder as the sound of thundering footsteps made its way through the caves.

"Go," Agni said.

He lay still, unmoving. He was gone.

I was numb. I couldn't feel anything. Pele's cries woke me from my stupor, and the need to survive kicked in. I had to keep her safe.

I stood on shaky legs and left through the secret exit.

The way was dark. Pele wailed. I shushed and rocked her, hoping she wouldn't give us away.

Armor clanked and shouts echoed off the walls. They were on my trail. I shushed Pele with more urgency, but she couldn't understand that this was a life-or-death situation. I picked up the pace. To make it out of this alive, I had to be fast.

I exited the tunnel on the other side of the mountain. There was a village down below, their pastures nearby. I had to make it there, seek their protection. But there was no cover until the village itself.

I took off at a sprint, not wanting to waste any more time. I held Pele close to my chest so she wouldn't be too jostled by my movements. When I was halfway to the pasture fence, I looked behind me. The king's men were racing after me, about a hundred yards back and gaining.

My heartrate picked up, blood rushing through my ears in time with the pounding of my feet. My breaths were shallow and fast. I focused my attention on the fence in front of me, starting the fire as hot as I could. I didn't have time to launch myself over it. Instead, I would burn it. I ran through the fire, muttering a protection spell.

I turned and faced the fence, building the fire I had started into a wall of flames. It wouldn't hold them for long, but at least it would give me some time to get Pele to safety. It was becoming clear that I wouldn't make it. I had to do everything in my power to make sure Pele had a future. I forced down the emotions that bubbled up when I thought of not being there for her. I would not allow myself to cry.

I was wasting time I didn't have. I hurried through the pastures and made my way into the town. As I ran, I searched for yards with signs of kids, such as toys. I found a promising one in the middle of the village.

In the scant front yard sat a hand-carved rocking horse small enough for a toddler. I ran to the door and knocked, trying to convey urgency to those inside. A woman with sandy-brown hair answered the door, alarm in her features. A toddler, a boy with her hair and green eyes, peeked around her legs.

I held onto Pele with one hand and pulled the knot of the sling over my head with the other. I took a moment to hold my baby girl, to kiss her, to say goodbye. Pele's tears started again, quieter this time. It was as if she knew what was coming.

"Mama loves you, Pele. Never forget that." I shoved her into the woman's unsuspecting arms. Pele wailed more violently, not used to strangers.

The woman tried to hand her back, but I refused. "Take care of her. Her name is Pele. If anyone asks, she's yours. When you can, try to get to the village on the other side of the mountain. It's probably in ashes, but try to find a large leather-bound book with blank yellowed pages and a ruby-eyed dragon on the cover. There should be one in any house. Find one that is mostly intact and give it to her, along with this letter, on her eighteenth birthday, the sixth of June. The year is on the letter." I stared at the woman, needing her to understand and accept before the king's men found me. I could hear them getting closer in their search.

She shook her head, concern in her eyes. "I can't."

"You must. I don't have time. I've got to go."

Before the woman could protest, I was off, running toward the far gate of the village, my vision blurred by tears. I wouldn't see her again. That much I knew. I could only hope I had chosen the right family, one that would love her and take care of her. She was safer with them than she would be with me.

I couldn't see through the tears anymore. I heard shouts, and hands grabbed my arms. I fought hard, but they pulled a blindfold over my face. It didn't matter. I wouldn't have been able to fight back with fire through the tears, anyway.

They forced me to my knees, kicking and screaming. I stopped struggling when a blade pressed into my neck.

"Where's the baby?" a gruff voice asked.

"What baby?"

He pressed the blade harder against my throat. "Don't play coy."

I remained silent. I could only pray the woman I had left Pele with would do the same. My heart felt like an abyss I was falling into deeper and deeper. I couldn't breathe.

"Don't bother with the baby," a bored voice said. "It can't get its powers without a parent around, so it's no threat to us. This is the last of the fire-starters. Kill her, and the whole line will be dead, just like the dragons."

I swallowed thickly. They had killed all the dragons? Pele would grow up in a very different world than I had. She would only know one season: winter.

As if in answer to my thought, the familiar cold, tickling sensation of a fluffy snowflake touched my cheek and melted.

"Snow? In July?" said one of the men before me.

"It's probably some trick of the fire-starter. If you kill her, I'm sure it will stop," said the bored voice again.

I swallowed down a bitter laugh. I would not correct them. They didn't deserve to know what they had done. They didn't deserve the chance for preparation.

The knife pressed harder into my throat, making it difficult to breathe. My head spun. I relaxed, closing my eyes. Pele was safe. That was all that mattered.

Riding the Lightning

Jess Reece

Tempest Knight plucked a clod of dirt from the ground, crumbling it between her fingers. Huge white clouds gathered on the horizon, and Tempest thought she saw a brief flash of jagged white light. The clouds never seemed to come close enough anymore. *How many days has it been since it rained?* The liquid silver of her eyes sparkled as resolve filled her heart. It had nearly killed her last time, but it was time to ride the lightning again.

Tempest returned to her air-cycle, trailing her fingers over the stylized hammer etched into the metal next to the word *Mjolnir*. Copper and steel gleamed brightly, accented by leather, soot, and travel grime. She grinned. This machine was a labor of love, one she'd personally assembled down to every last nut and bolt.

Rewarded with the *hiss-rumble* of the steam-powered motor roaring to life, she checked the far horizon once more. *There!* Another flash. Lowering her goggles, she cranked the gear that raised the cycle into the air. The familiar sting of wind-chapped cheeks thrilled her as her heart raced in time with the engine between her knees.

Her wild nature had estranged her from her family long ago. *Be proper,* they said. *Be ladylike,* they demanded. *Be normal,* they begged. But how could she when she had fire in her veins and a storm in her soul that was never quenched?

Victorian conventions held no appeal for her—not the way the sky called to her soul, and *never* the way that billowing thunderheads drew her like a magnet to a lodestone. Tempest patted the capacitor tube strapped behind her. The ingenious device had been developed by prominent scientists, then promptly stolen by air-pirates, who used the technology to harness and sell, quite literally, lightning in a bottle.

The privateers she had fallen in with months ago were much more bloodthirsty than she'd bargained for, but getting out from under Captain Augustus Penn's thumb had proven tricky. Once she'd captured enough megajoules, she would be released from her thrall and become a freeman once more.

Just a little bit more. That's what she told herself these days. *A little more.*

Sunlight brightened the uppermost curves of the looming clouds, while inky darkness possessed the underside. Tempest bared her teeth in a triumphant grin. *This* was the thrill she lived for. *This* was what her mother and grandmother could never understand with their corsets, lace gloves, and oh-so-proper manners.

From the northeast, a shadow appeared—no more than a vague black dot against the gray clouds. Tempest frowned.

Pirates!

She'd be damned if she was going to lose the first chance she'd had in weeks of filling her empty canisters. Rumors of storm dragons disappearing had grown rampant, and the lack of rain seemed to support the idea. Not everything she'd been taught in primary school about dragons was true; then again, most lessons from those days were useless to her now.

She gunned the engine, and the cycle zoomed through the sky as if powered by Thor himself. *It's time to capture some lightning.* Tempest maneuvered her air-cycle in behind the airship, stifling an irritated snort that these pirates still flew the Jolly Roger. A throwback to the days of swashbucklers sailing the seven seas, it seemed a bit outdated in this day and age, with steam engines, airships, and Her Majesty's Navy controlling the skies.

Ahead, great canvas fins extended laterally from the sides of the ship. Sails billowed up and out from three large masts, and even through her soot-stained goggles, Tempest could make out the men climbing the rigging and hauling out the canisters to capture the lightning. Thunder boomed above, and she felt the shudder of it clear through the chassis as she steered the cycle under the airship and out of sight of the pirates.

Despite the protection provided by the belly of the ship, rain pelted her sideways and gusts of wind threatened to unseat her. Lightning flashed again, closer this time. Pursing her lips into a scowl, she flipped the switch to extend the cycle's mechanical wings. Tempest caught the creak and groan of leather and steel as they opened, supported by steel ribs and copper sinew. In moments like this, she could almost imagine herself riding the back of a *real* dragon, like the heroes in children's books.

Those fanciful thoughts were driven from her head as white-hot lightning slammed into the airship above her. The mainmast, topped with a conductive cap designed to absorb the electricity, should have channeled it into the reinforced canisters in the ship's hold, but something was seriously wrong.

The airship rocked hard to port, tilting precariously, as if hit by a rogue wave. Throttling back to avoid a collision, she watched, stunned, as it continued to list. Over the shrieking wind and rain, she thought she heard men screaming. Another bolt of lightning slammed into the ship, striking the starboard planks and splintering them apart as if they were nothing more than matchsticks.

An internal explosion rocked the ship, sending out a mighty shockwave that caught Tempest before she could maneuver to safety. As she tumbled through the sky, the left aileron snapped off, sending her into a dizzying spin. Unable to tell up from down, she plummeted out of the sky, her terrified scream ripped away by the wind.

She was falling.
A ship was falling with her.
No, above her.
Falling, endlessly falling.

Tempest gasped, sitting up straight and staring around in confusion. The last thing she remembered was the explosion. Leaping to her feet, she searched for rubble from the ship.

"Where the bloody hell am I?"

If the pirates had somehow captured her, they'd done a wondrous job addling her brains. Tempest felt her skull for signs of injury, but only found long strands of silver hair that had pulled free of her braid. Her goggles and aviator cap were long gone, though aside from a rip in her leather jacket, everything else seemed intact.

Thick walls of fog surrounded her. The mottled gray rock beneath her feet revealed little in the way of helpful information. Edging forward, she waved her hands to try clearing away the mist, surprised by how cold it was. Droplets settled onto her skin like fairy kisses, and she thought she saw shadows moving in the dim light. Taking one more step into the cloying fog, she tipped forward into nothingness, right over the edge of a hidden cliff.

Before Tempest could so much as squeak in terror, a massive clawed hand caught her in midair. As if she weighed no more than a feather, she was set safely back upon the rock ledge. She gaped at the enormous swirling, electric-blue eyes that stared down into her own. Then her gaze traveled down a ridged snout to sharp, bony jaws that reminded her of a tropical parrot she'd seen once at a circus that had had tail feathers longer than her arm.

"D-d-d-dragon," she stuttered, stumbling away from the deadly looking maw. She promptly landed on her tailbone. "Ow!"

"Are you injured?"

"Who said that?" Tempest whipped her head left and right to determine where the rich, deep, masculine voice had come from.

"We asked if you were hurt?"

Tempest eyed the muzzle of the dragon nudging her leg, expecting at any moment to be chewed up and swallowed down its gullet. Drawing away from the bony snout, she stifled another scream. The dragon blew a warm gust of air over her, sending her tangled locks puffing out from her shoulders.

"Are . . . are you *talking* to me?"

"Of course we are talking to you."

Tempest fought the urge to reach out and stroke the dragon's leathery skin, wondering deep in her mind if she were hallucinating. Maybe she was lying in a hospital somewhere, deep in a comatose state. Or maybe she had crossed the abyss into death.

"You are not dead."

"Stop talking inside my head!" she snapped at him and was rewarded with the distinct impression of bemusement. "Where am I?"

"You are in our home, of course."

"But where is home?"

When she received no answer, Tempest got to her feet, surveying her surroundings once more. So far, only the dragon's head and clawed hand were visible through the thick fog coating the rocky ledge. She sighed in frustration, turning back around.

"I only see you."

"We do not understand."

"Okay, let's start over. I am Tempest. Tempest Knight." She frowned as she suppressed the urge to hold out her hand. "Do you have a name?"

"We are pleased to meet you, Tempest Tempest Knight. We are called Nefelibata."

"Nefeli-what?"

"Nefelibata."

"Nefelibata. Okay. Do you know what happened to the air-cycle I was riding?"

"You fell from the sky, Tempest Tempest Knight."

"No, that's not—my name is just Tempest Knight," she corrected, chewing her lower lip. "Bollocks. I was hoping it had been saved too. What about the pirate airship?"

"It was destroyed."

"Where are we?"

"We will show you."

A strange creaking filled the air, and the stone under her boots rumbled as if something quite large were moving about. Tempest was nearly knocked over by a great *whoosh* of air as the foggy mist cleared. She gasped. They were perched on the uppermost peak of a vast mountain range.

"We are in the Southern Fells."

"The Southern Fells? But that's over three hundred miles from London!"

"We know not of miles, but the Southern Fells are our home."

Tempest plopped down of her own accord, all the wind knocked out of her sails, so to speak. She was hundreds of miles from home, was with a dragon, and had no way to get back. Bloody hell, she'd been in some tight pinches before, but this one beat them all.

"Why did you save me?" She turned to Nefelibata, craning her neck as the dragon revealed itself.

Nefelibata's wingspan had to be as wide as the lateral fins on the pirates' ship. Sapphire-blue skin stretched between bony struts supported by powerful muscles, tendons, and ligaments. It dawned on her that it was those enormous wings that had blown away the shroud of fog. Curved horns—at least as big around as her thigh— swept back from his sleek face, and row after row of scaly electric-blue spikes bristled along the spine clear down to his tail. Those swirling electric eyes stared into hers, mesmerizing her where she stood.

"We are sick. We are dying. We need your help, Tempest Knight."

"You keep saying *we*, but I don't understand!"

"It is easier for us to show you."

Before she quite knew what was happening, Nefelibata nosed his great head forward until the curved beakish snout rested against her own forehead. A flurry of images crowded Tempest's mind, and she would have fallen if it weren't for the unusual connection between them. Initially, the images made no sense, but soon they formed a visual story of sorts.

*Storm clouds taller than mountains. Rumbling thunder. Many voices in her mind all at once. Dragonets play fight, flexing their growing wings and chasing each other head over tail as they race through the sky. Elder dragons open their great maws to spew forth bright blue-white fire—no, not fire, lightning. Broody mother dragons—*gallinas *is the word that flows through her mind—guard clutches of sapphire-blue eggs covered in electric-blue speckles, growling at any dragon who dares to come too close to their nest.*

The scene shifts.

Adult gallinas *and tiercels—male dragons—sweep through the sky, bellowing to each other and spewing the lightning coveted so desperately by airpirates. Ships, too many to count, appear from several directions within the clouds. The storm dragons scatter, camouflaging themselves in the billowing clouds. Curiosity gets the better of them, however, as these ships do not behave like others that have been caught in the great thunderheads.*

A great, collective cry of pain goes up as a harpoon whips out from the prow of one ship, piercing clean through the ribs of the closest dragon.

The pain is shared among the others. Even the broody mothers and retired elders feel the sting, the flow of blood from the wound, and as one, they cry out for the death of their brother. One by one, more harpoons are released, slaughtering the dragons in the sky. Few escape. Even fewer survive.

Several airships break off from the others to hunt the nesting mothers and destroy the egg clutches. Just as quickly as they appeared, the fleet of ships withdraws, going to ground to butcher the dead and dying dragons. Grief, palpable and devastating, beats in the hearts of those dragons lucky enough to flee.

Tempest yanked herself away from Nefelibata, dropping to her knees to retch. The awful images were burned into her brain, and she knew she'd forever be haunted by them. Tempest had recognized the crests emblazoned on the sides of the airships. Storm dragons hadn't just disappeared mysteriously, as Her Majesty's Imperial Defense Force would have the citizens of Great Britain believe.

They were directly responsible for their slaughter.

"God in heaven . . . what . . . why . . ." Her voice faltered as she looked up at Nefelibata, tears streaming down her cheeks.

The dragon nuzzled her once more, and Tempest jerked back, unwilling to connect mentally again without collapsing. Instead of horrifying memories, Tempest was flooded with loving warmth. Staring into the beautiful swirling eyes, she reached out a hand to caress the bony beak, awed by the enormous power exuded by the massive creature.

"Your kind has hunted us for centuries, stealing the life's breath from our very bodies. We have declined, almost to the point of extinction. Our dragonets die before they reach full dragonhood. Our mothers grieve clutches that never quicken. Our fledged males have no mates. Something must be done."

"What do you need me to do?"

"You were attempting to stop the marauding airship, Tempest Knight."

"Oh, I don't know if—"

"We need a champion, Tempest Knight. We need to stop the theft of lightning from the storm dragons."

Hours later, Tempest found herself turning Nefelibata's words over in her mind. Shame washed over her once again at her failure to correct the dragon's perception of her proximity to the pirates. Nefelibata assumed that she had been there to interfere with the capture of the storm's lightning, but Tempest wasn't honorable enough to reveal the truth. If only she could get word to her niece, she'd perhaps be able to come up with a plan. Hettie was premier veterinarian to the queen's own dragon, Xymmos. If anyone could help, *she* would be able to. As it was, Tempest was completely out of her element—trying to end the extermination of dragons, storm dragons in particular, was surely next to impossible for her alone.

"You are awake, Tempest Knight."

"You can just call me Tempest, you know." She smiled despite the strange situation she'd found herself in.

"We are hungry. Do you need to feed?"

She cringed. "To feed" just sounded so *distasteful*. However, her belly was grumbling plaintively, and her muscles were sore from lying on a slab of cold stone, even if Nefelibata had wrapped his tail around for her to use as a pillow.

Tempest smiled. She had never imagined that dragon skin would have such a sharp, metallic smell to it. Not unpleasant exactly, but definitely distinct, almost like the burnt-ozone scent of lightning itself.

"Yes, I am hungry. I'm not sure where I could find some food, though, without my air-cycle."

"We will find you something to eat, never fear."

She harrumphed. Fear? She was simply at the mercy of an enormous dragon perched on a mountaintop, hundreds of miles from home. What could there be to fear?

"Are you ready, Tempest?"

"Ready? Ready for what—"

Nefelibata scooped her up, depositing her on his back, just ahead of the powerful muscles of his wings. The spiny protrusions along his back were absent here, providing a comfortable place to sit—at least it would have, if she'd been calm enough to appreciate the experience.

Crouching, he launched himself straight up, catching an updraft expertly. Tempest clung to the dragon's back, squeezing her eyes tight, and let loose a scream the pitch of which was probably only capable of being heard by dogs. Wind whooshed past her face, tugging so hard at her hair that she thought it might be ripped from her scalp. Her cheeks burned, and her teeth hurt from clenching her jaw.

"You are safe, Tempest. We will not allow you to fall."

She peeked her eyes open the teeniest bit. Gawking at her surroundings, she allowed the soaring scenery to fill her heart with awe. This was not at all like riding her cycle through the sky. This was better!

Tempest felt the dragon smile in her mind. Nefelibata pumped his wings, gaining altitude surprisingly fast. The air around them grew colder, and still he rose higher in the sky. She gripped his neck with her thighs, clutching the rigid dorsal spines as if she were holding onto a horse's reins. Just as her lungs began to labor for air, Nefelibata twisted into a tight barrel roll and dove downward.

Too shocked to scream, too frightened to breathe, Tempest held on for dear life as they plummeted out of the sky. Tears blurred her eyes as the wind burned her skin. Her knuckles were white and her belly had lodged itself in her throat, but this was by far the most exhilarating thing she had ever experienced.

What would her mother say if she could see Tempest now?

"Wait! We're too close! You have to stop!" Tempest screamed as the ground rushed up at them.

Just yards from certain death, Nefelibata pulled out of the dizzying dive, gliding above the earth with lazy strokes of his wings. As he swept upward over the ridge of another hill, Tempest saw a small herd of wild sheep. Hunger, intense and painful, rumbled through her belly. For a moment, she was horrified by the primal urge to tear into the tender woolly bodies below that the dragon was projecting into her mind.

"The sheep are not for you, little one."

"Don't laugh at me, you crazy dragon!" She slapped his side affectionately.

Nefelibata backwinged, letting her slide safely down his foreleg. As soon as her feet touched the ground, he launched himself upward again. She watched his sleek blue body circle overhead, then swoop down, plucking an unfortunate sheep out of the flock. He settled down far enough away that she didn't have to watch him tear into the still-bleating animal, and she turned her attention to foraging for something to eat.

Bending over, she found dandelion, chickweed, sorrel, and wild onion. Grinning, she thought of her grandmother and the many summers they had spent foraging just like this in the wild hills behind her cottage. They were dear memories, ones she didn't allow herself to think on often. Quickly eating her makeshift breakfast, she waited for Nefelibata to finish his own meal.

The dragon padded over to where Tempest sat in the grass, and she marveled at his powerful muscles and brilliant eyes. How many times had she collected the unique lightning from these very creatures? How had she never considered the sources of the electricity she effectively stole from them? If there hadn't been such a shortage of electric power at the hands of the company assigned by the Queen's advisor, there wouldn't have been a reason to steal from the dragons at all. Shaking her head, she looked down at the ground until Nefelibata stopped in front of her.

"Tempest, the pirates must be stopped. I am confident you will save us. What will we do?"

"I've been thinking about that." Tempest crushed some grass in her fist. "I think I know someone that can help."

If she felt a little guilty about using the word *help*, Tempest shoved it away as best as she could. She was desperate, and there was only one person she could think of to try to save what remained of the storm dragons. After explaining her idea to Nefelibata, she waited anxiously for his reply.

"I will take you to this place, Tempest Knight. Together we will end the slaughter of my kin."

Less than a full day later, Tempest was toasting her reunion with Captain Penn. Nefelibata turned out to be surprisingly helpful—and resourceful—in getting the equipment that Tempest needed to contact the captain. Now Gus sat in front of her, tapping his fingers on the worn table between them.

"What is it that's so special, you dragged me from my bunk at all hours of the night?" he growled.

"Gus, it's not even noon."

"Might as well be night." He sniffed and downed his whiskey. "Tell me what you want, and be quick about it."

"You've been getting robbed." She shrugged, getting to her feet. "But if you're too busy to find out the how and why . . . well then, I guess I'll be on my way."

"Robbed!" He leaped up, grabbing her arm. "Oi! You ain't leaving here until you explain yourself, Knight."

"Someone is killing storm dragons. Entire clans of them, in fact, including clutches. Without dragons—"

"There'd be no lightning to catch from them stormies," he murmured, sitting back down.

"Exactly. I know it's not you and your crew. Nor is it the *Raider*, the *Black Revenge*, or the *Brazen Strumpet*. Now, we need to find a way to stop the marauders before they hunt the dragons into extinction." She propped her boots up on the table. "They always attack them during the end of the season, Gus."

"That's just around the corner. What do you propose, then, lass?" He eyed her with something akin to suspicion.

"Something to benefit us both, Gus. There are only two days left in the season, though, so we have to hurry."

She refilled their whiskey, laying out the idea she'd concocted in the last twenty-four hours. Gus was difficult to convince at first, especially given her demands, but the prospect of single-handedly cornering the lightning market was alluring enough that he finally signed the paper she placed in front of him. He brought in his crew to explain their plans. There was some grumbling, but most were excited by the idea of not only making a last run for lightning but stopping the marauders who threatened to kill their livelihood altogether.

Tempest excused herself, tucking a small roll of parchment into a leather pouch at her belt and promising to return the following morning. She made one last stop in town before directing the carriage she'd hired to drop her off outside the market, where she hurried along a goat path to meet Nefelibata. The clever dragon had hidden himself in the depths of a small loch, his shimmering blue skin perfectly camouflaged by the water.

"We are happy that you have returned, Tempest."

She was surprised to find his words were tinged with affection. Not only that, but in the short time she had spent with him, she'd developed an affection for him as well. The dragon surged up onto the bank, shaking off water much as a dog would, and she laughed at the comical sight.

"Enough playing around now, good sir," she said, trying to

sound severe. "I need to tell you about my meeting with Captain Penn."

"We are indebted to you, Tempest Knight."

"Well, don't thank me yet," she warned. "We still need to stop the marauders."

Nefelibata helped Tempest onto his back once more, and soon they were flying through the sky, heading back to the dragon's aerie atop the Southern Fells. Her eyes nearly bugged out when she spotted two more dragons waiting for them on the mountain. Both were similar in size to Nefelibata, but one was a much deeper blue, almost indigo, with bright turquoise eyes. Tempest slid down Nefelibata's foreleg, and he bowed his head to the dark blue dragon. She followed suit, sensing that this new dragon was an alpha of some kind.

"We are pleased to meet you, Tempest Knight. We are called Brumous. Nefelibata tells us that you are a heroic champion to our kind. We are in your debt."

In Tempest's mind, Brumous's voice sounded distinctly feminine, and Tempest wondered about the hierarchy of the storm dragons. Her thoughts were interrupted when Brumous knelt, dipping her head to the ground at Tempest's feet. Tempest stumbled backward, speechless and feeling even more like a fraud than before. She did not deserve this noble creature's respect, let alone gratitude.

"Please, Your, ah, Excellency," Tempest stammered. "Thank you, but really, it's not necessary."

All three dragons started speaking at once in that peculiar way of theirs, and Tempest clapped her hands to her ears. It was like having three radios blasting at the same time, without being able to turn the volume down. Nefelibata noted her distress and hushed the others.

"It is time to go."

Brumous let out a trilling bugle, the first verbal sound Tempest had heard from any of the storm dragons, and she watched in wonder as several blue dots circled down out of the sky. They did not land but instead maintained a holding pattern of dips, dives, and spectacular aerial acrobatics. Tempest had the impression that these were younger dragons, not much older than dragonets, and were all that remained beyond the elders who had joined Nefelibata and a few safely hidden clutches that she'd been told about. Her heart constricted. Such young fighters—with so little experience, how could they possibly be successful against an entire *fleet* of airships?

Seated between Nefelibata's shoulders, Tempest tucked her hair under a new aviator cap, pulling her goggles down to protect her eyes. The dragon bunched his muscles, and the next moment, they were airborne. A now-familiar tickle flipped her belly over, but she was prepared for it this time. They joined the flight of storm dragons, forming a V like she'd seen countless birds do throughout her lifetime.

Up ahead, Gus Penn's ship, the *Trésor*, dropped out of the clouds, flying its signature red flag with a stylized white lightning bolt. The dragons adjusted their flight pattern to accommodate the airship, and Tempest noticed, with some relief, that the airship had her port and starboard cannons readied for battle.

Lightning lit up the sky, and thunder boomed all around them. To her left and right, the dorsal spines of the storm dragons lit up a bright, electric blue, and a singular sort of hum filled her ears, like that of a sparking electrode. Between her knees, she felt the rumble of Nefelibata's indrawn breath, and a heartbeat later, the dragon belched forth a great zigzagging bolt of lightning. The blue-white fire arced outward, to be joined by lightning bolts spewed from the mouths of the other dragons. It was an astonishing sight to behold, and Tempest found her heart swelling with the enormous beauty of the spectacular display.

A blaring alarm rang out from the *Trésor*, and Tempest leaned to the side to look beyond the prow of the pirate ship. A small fleet—at least two ships for each dragon—had dropped out of the thickest cloud cover and was racing straight for them. Splitting off into two flights, the dragons pumped their wings, engaging several of the marauder ships. Jagged lightning split the sky in twenty places at once, their bright blue fingers smashing into wooden hulls as easily as did the *Trésor*'s cannons.

The fighting was intense, and it was all Tempest could do to remain on Nefelibata's back. His rumbling breath, followed by lightning fire, was so instinctive to her now, she knew before he even turned his head which target would be next.

A terrible keening screeched inside her mind, followed by heart-crushing grief. To her left, the body of a dragon fell from the sky, a harpoon through its chest.

"We have to help!" she shouted, and Nefelibata veered sideways.

All at once, a ship—*a marauder ship*—appeared behind them. Tempest tried to warn Nefelibata, but it was too late. The silver glint of a harpoon whipping through the air was her only warning before the barbed steel pierced his hide. Mind-numbing pain racked her body, transmitted to her through their telepathic link. The dragon faltered as he tried to regain altitude, but the harpoon had pierced the leading edge of his wing, pinning it to his side.

Tempest scooted her rear end backward, reaching out to loosen the harpoon. It wasn't embedded deeply, but if she didn't get it free, Nefelibata wouldn't be able to fly. The damn weapon was just out of reach, and she slid even farther back, forcing herself to ignore the spinning skyscape around her.

Two more inches, then one more inch, and she almost had it.

"Aha! Got you!"

Tempest gripped the harpoon, yanking it out of his hide. Nefelibata roared in pain, but his wing was finally free to fully extend. The abrupt combination of her ripping out the steel barb, the dragon extending his wing, and his sudden lurch upright unseated Tempest completely. With a small surprised squeak, she lost her grip. Several bolts of dragon lightning hit the marauder airship simultaneously, splintering it into thousands of pieces that rained down with her.

Tempest was falling.

A ship was falling above her.

No, around her.

But this time, no dragon on Earth would be fast enough to save her.

Makara's Treasure

Kimberly Gail

I swore under my breath, cursing the heat in the crowded fishing village. The feel of my gown clinging to my sweat-soaked skin repulsed me. The rich, beautiful purple silk would never be clean again. I had never felt such an oppressive heat before. It was my first trip to the ocean, and it was nothing like I'd imagined. There were no sandy beaches or cool ocean breezes.

But worse than the heat was the smell. It took great strength and determination for me to keep from gagging. I had never realized that creatures of the sea had such a foul stench.

Never one to let such things stop me, I inhaled a deep breath, forcing my nose and lungs to acclimate to the foreign surroundings. I would happily endure whatever came my way as I drew closer to the treasure I sought. My collection was already grander than any other. My trove contained many rare jewels that others had never dared dream even existed. I could almost taste the envy of those who gazed upon my treasures. I imagined the stench of that village to be the scent of jealousy radiating from my rivals, and I relished it as I drew in another deep breath.

I held that breath for a count of ten in an effort to still my annoyance over something far more aggravating than either the heat or the smell. It threatened to cross over into anger, and I had learned in my years hunting treasure that anger rarely got you what you wanted.

I calmed myself before repeating my request to the captain of the fishing vessel I wished to hire.

The creases of the old fisherman's wrinkles furrowed into what seemed impossible depths as he howled laughter in my face.

"You'll find no one willing to take you there," he crowed.

"Is your vessel not capable enough, or is it your own skills as a captain you lack faith in?"

My barb found its mark and stung. The old man's smile faded. "It's not any man or vessel that's the worry, young Miss. 'Tis the fact that trouble is all you'll find out there when you trespass into the realm of Pratish, Lord of the Sea. There's not a man here crazy enough to sail out to meet his wrath."

"I've learned of many extraordinary creatures in my lifetime, but a vengeful sea god is not among them." I laughed. "You are a fool to pass up the kind of money I'm offering just because of some nonsensical superstition." With that remark, my men and I walked off to find someone less foolish to ferry us out to sea.

Unfortunately, he was not the only such fool I encountered. All morning, my men and I approached different captains, offering ridiculous sums to carry us to our destination. But money, it seemed, could not compete with fear for most men.

It was nearly afternoon when we found the owner of a vessel willing to accept our offer, which we had tripled by then. That was how we ended up sailing out to sea on a rickety old *machwa*. Such small vessels were not meant for a voyage so far, but as it was our only option, we were forced to take it. When it came time to sail, the boat's captain stayed behind, sending only his oarsmen to man the boat.

As I sat upon the splintered boards of the decrepit little boat I'd procured, I willed myself not to mind. Instead, I looked ahead toward where my prize was rumored to lie, somewhere beneath the shimmering waves.

My thoughts of glory were disrupted by the sound of the

machwa's oarsmen muttering nervously under their breath to one another in Hindi. They whispered of danger, of curses, of the wrath of the Lord of the Sea. I rolled my eyes and let out a huff of disgust.

"Shouldn't you be attending to your duties, not gossiping like old grandmothers?" I admonished. I had no patience and even less respect for foolish men with foolish notions.

It took hours to reach the deep sea in the *machwa*. The sun was beginning to set as we arrived. The waves shone like gold and amber in its glow. A chill raced from my head to my toes, and I knew for sure: my treasure would be there.

The oarsmen huddled together under the makeshift roof, cowering. I rolled my eyes and slung a slew of Hindi curses at their fear. With a huff, I threw my long dark braid over my shoulder and looked at my two loyal servants, Dilan and Karnan. Their expressions mirrored my own feelings.

They were fine men, nearly as valuable to me as my treasured jewels. Not in the same ways, of course. Although, they were spectacular to look at, with strong muscles that rippled beneath their tawny skin and matching dark green eyes. Those eyes themselves made my men a rarity among our people. But no, it was not their beauty but rather their unwavering loyalty and dedication to me that made them valuable.

Karnan readied the netted cage, which had been expertly crafted by Dilan with fibers that matched the colors of the sea to make it nearly invisible once submerged.

I prepared the bait.

I removed my own jewels—exquisite diamonds and pearls— from around my neck and tied them among the net. Beside them, I placed a gilded hand mirror, its surface so polished, it shone as bright as the setting sun. As my men lowered the net into the sea, I sat down once more upon that splintered bench and began to strum the most beautiful tune upon my lyre.

I had heard the rumors, listened to the stories, and studied all the lore I could get my delicate hands on. I knew everything there was to know about this particular treasure, and I had come prepared with everything I needed to acquire it. Each piece had been carefully selected to help me trap a mermaid.

Yes, the treasures I sought were ones not of gold or jewels but of creatures—rare, beautiful, magnificent creatures. I had grown so bored with ordinary treasures. Jewels, coins, money, art—even romantic trysts—had all lost their appeal. Such common things, really. Things anyone could get their hands on. But creatures of legend? Now there was a rare and glorious thing to collect, to hoard away for myself.

My trove was full of them. A glorious menagerie that included fairies, gnomes, satyrs, imps, unicorns, and even a centaur. Those were but a few of the jewels in my cache. But I was missing one of the rarest and most beautiful gems of all. My collection still needed a mermaid.

And finally, there I was, within reach. The *machwa* floated directly over the legendary kingdom of the merfolk. We rocked about on the waves as we sat on the shimmering surface of Kshithij. A smile spread wide across my face as I relished that I had dared go to a place some feared and most didn't believe existed.

Dilan expressed concern that we might be in for a long wait, but I could feel it deep within my core that my new treasure was near. From my research, I had gleaned that there was always one of their kind who flitted about the surface, dreaming of drier places. One who kept themselves isolated and, therefore, always at risk. One who would do anything, give anything, and yes, risk anything to escape the depths.

I was right, of course. We did not have to wait long before a tug on the line let us know something, or someone, had swum into our net. My men moved fast, pulling the ropes to lift the cage from the water. Harsh warnings shouted at the oarsmen had them crawling from their corner, and they helped heave the contraption onto the boat.

I inched closer, slowly. At first, all I saw was the straining muscles in the men's backs as they worked. Then they moved, and I saw her. My eyes, brown as the earth, met hers: wide, frightened, and the same piercing blue-green of the sea. She was the most beautiful creature I had ever seen. Hair like spun gold, turquoise eyes, flesh as smooth and pale as pearl.

And her tail! Oh, how the scales of her tail shimmered like amethyst in the growing light of the moon. She would be the prize jewel of my grand menagerie.

The men, both my servants and the boat's crew, gathered round, pushing each other out of the way in an effort to get closer. They were captivated by her beauty. I snarled at them and demanded they get back. This was my treasure. Someday, I would be ready to show her off to the world, to make them all envy me and what I possessed. But in that moment, I wanted her all to myself. I didn't want them even looking upon my jewel.

I saw her fear and desperation, and I tried to pay it little heed. Every treasure in my trove had reeked of such things in the beginning. It would fade with time, and she would learn to settle in, just as they had.

But something in her eyes struck me, so I decided I should do something to try and soothe her. I grabbed up my lyre once more and played a calming tune.

I was overcome by the music. The notes entranced me every bit as much as my beautiful new jewel. I was so lost in the moment, the melody, and her bewitching eyes that I did not feel the presence of someone new.

Not until I heard the screams.

I turned and saw him then. The Lord of the Sea. Pratish. It was not a man I saw there, but a god. And not a benevolent one. He held one of the oarsmen tightly against his body with one arm. I stared, frozen with a terror unlike any I had ever felt, as he reached up and grasped the man's face in his free hand. His nails were long and sharp, like claws. Blood appeared in half-moon slits as he used those claws to dig into the oarsman's flesh. There was no hesitation as he pulled his hand sharply away from the man's head, taking the skin of his face with it.

They had been right. All those superstitious fools had been so very right not to come here. I looked about desperately for somewhere to go, but there was nowhere. I was every bit as trapped as the mermaid in the cage next to me.

I looked to her then. Fear no longer lived in her eyes. No, now they were a raging sea filled with danger. I started to scuttle backward, to get away from her. To get away from them both.

A loud growl drew my attention back to the sea god. Dilan, my loyal servant, clutched a harpoon and began to thrust it at the creature. But Pratish caught his arm, and in less than a second, tore the arm from his body. He flung it across the boat. I watched as it hit the deck and slid nearly within my reach. I began to dive for it, but suddenly a viselike grip caught my wrist.

A shrill scream tore from my throat. I knew I was about to suffer the same fate as my servant. But when I looked, it was not the Lord of the Sea who gripped my wrist, but the mermaid within the cage. I tried to pull away, but her grip was stronger than I could have imagined.

I closed my eyes so I would not have to witness the sea god's wrath. But nothing could block out the sounds as he tore through each and every one of the men on board the boat. Only when it was silent did I dare open my eyes.

Only one man still stood: Karnan. He was there, right before me, a barrier between me and the Lord of the Sea. Terror consumed me as he lunged for Pratish, only to be caught in his vicious grip. I felt my heart wrench in my chest. I could not lose my last treasured man.

I pulled against the grip on my wrist in an effort to reach him. It was no use, though; she was too strong. So I screamed out to the Lord of the Sea, "Stop! Do not hurt him."

Pratish hesitated. Karnan looked to me, and I could see in his beautiful eyes that, with only a signal from me, he would fight the monster holding him in death's grip. A tear ran down my cheek as I shook my head, advising him to do nothing.

"Why should I stop?" Pratish growled, his eyes roaming between me and the mermaid in the cage. I would have thought it difficult for one of their kind to move out of the water, but Pratish moved toward me on the blue scales of his tail with the graceful ease of a serpent. Karnan was still clutched in his grasp. My body trembled uncontrollably, and I felt a wet warmth trickle down my legs and spread across the silk of my gown as my bladder gave way to fear. I awaited death.

"Why?" he asked again.

"He is innocent in this, merely a servant under my orders. I am the one who deserves your wrath, not him."

Pratish looked at me with dark, threatening eyes. "You would offer your life in place of a servant's?"

I swallowed back my fear and nodded. "I would," I said weakly. Then with more conviction, "I do."

His grip upon Karnan increased until he dropped him, limp, before me. I dove toward him and placed my hand upon his chest. I felt the beat of his heart. He was unconscious, but alive.

Pratish's harsh glare claimed my gaze once more. "Tell me, human, why have you come here and captured one of my people?"

Under the powerful gaze of the sea god, I felt compelled to tell him everything, and so I did.

"I am a collector of rare creatures. At first, I simply wanted to possess them, but over time, they have all become more than that to me. Each jewel in my collection is in my care, my protection. These creatures—creatures like you—have come so close to disappearing from our world. Over the years, they have been hunted down and killed. Gathering them, locking them away in my trove, keeps them safe. As long as I collect and protect these rare gems, they will continue to exist."

Once I had finished speaking, he drew nearer, and again I expected death. Instead, he bent his tail and knelt before the cage. With hardly any effort, he tore it apart, freeing my treasured prize. She leaped for him, and he embraced her. His every feature softened, and in that moment, I saw beauty in his face, where before I had only seen a monster. He closed his dark eyes and rested his forehead against hers as he stroked her golden hair. I realized then that the beautiful creature I had captured was never my jewel to possess. She was the treasure of the Lord of the Sea.

His gaze turned to me as he released her, and once again that cruel harshness dominated his features. "I am ready for death," I said.

Death was not the punishment he delivered.

"You have spent your life enslaving others and fooling yourself that it was protection. Yet your offer of your life for your servant's proves you have the heart of a protector. Still, you must be punished."

He raised his hand, palm facing toward me, and spoke a single word.

Light. Nothing but light. Intense white light surrounded me with fiery heat. My eyes rolled back as my energy left me and I collapsed.

When I woke, I was underwater. Although I didn't feel it, I was sure I was drowning. In a panic, I raised my hand to clutch at my throat. What I saw before me, though, was not a hand. It was a fin, a large shimmering white fin.

I spun my head around to look at my body. As I did, I noticed a light following the motion. I blinked, and with it, the area around me began to darken. I opened one eye, and with it came the light. I opened the other, and the light intensified. My eyes glowed and lit the water around me.

Around my new body.

Like my fin, my body was covered in shimmering white scales. My tail—I had a tail! My tail was long and covered with sharp spikes along the top ridge. Along its length, there were glowing orbs. I stared at them in wonder for a moment before daring to move. My long body shot through the water at a reckless speed. I attempted to stop and went into an out-of-control roll.

"You will learn to control your new body in time."

The words came from behind me, and I carefully turned to see Pratish swimming there, his arm wrapped protectively around his mate's waist.

"I have handed down your punishment in the form of a gift,

Makara. I have given you what you have craved most: the gift of the rarest creature on Earth. With it comes a title and a responsibility."

There was one jewel I had known I would never find because it was extinct.

Pratish had just given it to me by turning me into a sea dragon.

Centuries later, I still lurk deep beneath Kshithij. I am Makara, Protector of the Merfolk, and I am my own living treasure.

Scorpions of Justice

Shannon McRoberts

Tamara gawked up at the imposing golden statue. A larger-than-life golden woman stood before her, holding an ankh with a scorpion perched on the top of its curve. *Why do the scorpion and ankh look familiar?*

A chilling wind blew through the cavernous room she stood in. Tamara shivered and unconsciously rubbed her arms. As her left hand touched her upper right arm, she immediately winced in pain. Pulling up the small sleeve, she found a scorpion traveling through the loop of an ankh emblazoned on her upper arm and shoulder.

Trying to remember how she had gotten the tattoo caused her head to ache. She remembered being out with her friends to celebrate her twenty-first birthday. It had been All Hallows' Eve, and Tamara and her friends had been on fall break. She remembered getting smashed at the local bar, and then someone had had the bright idea of going to a tattoo shop they had passed. Was that where she had gotten the tattoo? Whose idea had it been to go into that creepy place? Her memory was foggy as she tried to recall the sequence of events.

Tamara spun around to check if any of her friends were in the room. There was nothing there except for her and the statue. She glanced down and noticed she was dressed in something odd. It was a long white gown made of linen, adorned with golden threads and topped with a sheer overdress. An azure belt tied around her waist completed the ensemble. Her shoes were gone, leaving her feet bare. *How drunk did I get?*

Tamara had begun to walk toward what she assumed was the door when a voice called out behind her. Tamara paused and turned.

"Welcome, Initiate Tamara! Please, follow me." A tall blonde in a similar outfit had appeared and beckoned Tamara to follow her.

"Um, where am I? Why are you calling me 'initiate'?" Tamara questioned, refusing to follow the woman.

The woman smiled. "Gracious me! It has been so long since I had to address a newly chosen, I have forgotten my manners. My name is Aella, and I am your guide while you are here in the Temple of Serket. Your questions will be answered in due time, I promise. Please, follow me. We should not linger here."

The singsong quality of Aella's voice mixed with the urgency of her words enthralled Tamara. She followed the strange woman down a darkened corridor without another word. As Aella walked ahead, torches automatically flicked to life along the corridor. The gold-painted walls appeared to sparkle in the torchlight. The floor was a smooth, cool marble. Aella's and Tamara's bare feet made slight smacking noises as they moved down the corridor. Finally, Aella turned left and passed through a doorway into a room.

"Please sit down, Tamara." Aella motioned toward a chaise lounge.

Tamara, still captivated by Aella's voice, moved across the room to the chaise. She sat down on the chair, but she didn't recline. She looked around the room and noticed the decor was rather sparse. There were a few chaise lounges, a vase containing some kind of big leaves in the corner, and a vanity over against the wall farthest from her. Her gaze fell back to Aella, who now sat in the chaise next to her.

"So, can you tell me where I am?"

"The Temple of Serket, an interdimensional realm where all times coincide," Aella said matter-of-factly.

Tamara frowned. "You say that like I should know what it means."

Aella frowned. She got up, walked over to the vanity across the room, and waved her hands over the mirror.

From where Tamara sat, she could see some of the images Aella was studying. Though Aella's back was turned, Tamara didn't need to see her face to know she wasn't pleased; the disapproving tones Aella made told Tamara she wasn't amused by the images.

The mirror showed Tamara wandering into a tattoo shop, laughing with a group of friends. It went on to show Tamara circling past the various tattoo displays more than once, but she always came back to the ankh with a scorpion. Aella shook her head as the Tamara in the mirror inspected her new tattoo, right before the tattooist snapped his fingers, sending all the women into a deep sleep. The next image showed Tamara waking up in the Temple of Serket.

Aella waved her hand, causing the mirror to stop flashing. She put her head down on the vanity, her golden hair spilling over her shoulders.

"Are you okay, Aella?" Tamara asked, trying to figure out what she was doing. *Is it nap time?*

Aella straightened and turned back to face Tamara. A smile crossed Aella's lips, but her brown eyes were full of sadness. "It seems the universe has dealt me quite a hand. Why it would pick a young girl from the Earth dimension to be its newest angel of judgment is beyond me. So many individuals across the other dimensions train in hopes of being selected, but you wandered in with no knowledge and picked out the sacred ankh. Can you even tell me why you picked that design?"

Tamara shrugged. "Look, I was pretty hammered last night. I can't really say for sure why I picked it, but I feel like it called out to me. I was born on All Hallows' Eve, so the scorpion is my sun sign or whatever, and I've always thought scorpions were cool. That's most likely why I chose it. Also, I think I got a discount?"

Something Aella had mentioned before niggled at the back of Tamara's mind. "Wait, what did you say about angel of vengeance?"

"Not vengeance, judgment. As a vessel of Serket, you will travel the known dimensions and control your own sacred scorpions to judge those who we must judge. You will have the ability to heal the venom of creatures like scorpions, spiders, and snakes. You will also be able to move through time, both backward and forward, to aid in your ability to serve your judgment."

Tamara grimaced. "Yeah, I must still be really hungover. Traveling known dimensions? Controlling scorpions and judging those who must be judged? Time travel? I'm sorry, even if all of this is real, I don't have time for it. I have an algebra test on Tuesday that I didn't study for, and my parents will be really miffed if I fail. Can you just show me the way back to my dorm room?"

Aella's face turned red, and her nostrils flared. She balled her hands up into fists. "Is this a joke to you, Tamara? How could the sacred mark call out to such a selfish individual? Do you not understand the universe has chosen you? This is your sacred duty. Algebra will not help you. The universe does not care if your parents get mad at you for failing a remedial class. You were chosen to keep the balance of judgment in check. If you refuse this duty, the dimensions may plummet into chaos. Do you think algebra will save you from chaos?"

Tamara sat back in the chaise. Aella's anger permeated the room. "I guess if you put it like that, then no, algebra wouldn't help me."

Aella screamed and put her hands on top of her head, pulling at her hair. She looked up at the ceiling. "Goddess, why do you punish me so? Why have you chosen this lowly Earth-dimension dweller? She knows nothing of her duties! She is a disgrace to the sacred mark."

"Oh, hey, hold up there, blondie. I'm a disgrace? I didn't ask to be zapped to some weird temple, nor did I ask to be an angel of judgment. I also didn't say some goddess could brand me like a cow! I was perfectly fine minding my own business and having fun in my 'Earth dimension,' as you say. Seems to me, your angel picker is broken, and you should get a refund. Now send me home if I am such a disgrace and disappointment!"

The room flashed with a bright light, forcing Tamara to close her eyes. When the light dimmed, a woman resembling the golden statue in the cave room stood before both Aella and Tamara.

"My goddess Serket. You humble me by gracing us with your presence." Aella bowed.

"Get up, Aella. Spare me the pomp and circumstance. I grow weary of the old ways. Which is why I charged the universe to look for new blood." Serket turned to look at Tamara. The hint of a smile crossed Serket's lips as she realized Tamara stood gawking at her as if she weren't a goddess.

Tamara felt small in the presence of this woman who called herself Serket. She offered a small, shy wave.

Serket laughed. "No need to feel shy around me, Tamara. I am not as stuffy as Aella. Being an immortal teacher locked away in a faraway temple can cause one to become a little old-fashioned. I have begged her to take time off and travel the modern world. She could travel for a year and learn so much and only be gone from here for a day, what with her time travel powers. Yet she wishes to remain true to the time period from which she hails."

"I am not stuffy! There is nothing wrong with being proper. I certainly hope you do not send me more charges like Tamara here. She is undisciplined and ill-suited for this line of work."

Serket gave Aella a look of disapproval. "I chose Tamara myself because we need more recruits just like her."

Serket and Aella argued back and forth about Tamara's virtues. All the while, Tamara listened and watched these two women talk about her like she wasn't there. Finally, Tamara interjected.

"Hi, I'm right here. Can you both stop judging me like I'm not in the room? Look, Serket, I'm really honored you would go out of your way to choose me for your interdimensional league of super judgment heroes or whatever, but I think Aella is right. I'm not cut out for this kind of work."

Serket stopped and looked at Tamara. "Oh, but you are, dear. I have been watching you for some time now. You are ambitious and intelligent. What Aella does not understand about your preoccupation with your algebra test is why you need to pass said test. You have a goal of graduating college with a double major in three years, instead of four. If you do not do well in your classes, you will go off your timeline and miss your goal. And you have never missed your goals, have you, Tamara?"

Tamara looked down at her bare feet and chewed on her lip. "No, once I put my mind to a task, I complete it with everything I have."

"You also have a knack for being the problem solver in your group of friends. You tend to see solutions others do not, am I right?"

Tamara met Serket's gaze and held it. Serket's violet eyes glowed against her dark skin, and Tamara felt like Serket was looking into the very depths of her soul. "Yes, that's also true. Others know to come to me when they have a tough issue."

"Do you know what my vessels do for me, Tamara?"

Tamara shook her head. "No, I'm afraid I don't understand what your vessels do. What Aella told me seems rather incomprehensible."

"I see. She gave you the 'magic scorpion and time travel' speech, even though I have told her to stop using it, did she not? While it is true you will have magic at your command, the main function of my vessels is to help others in bad situations. We assist those who need vindication. We judge those who may have fallen through the cracks of mortal law. We also help those who have been wrongly accused gain fair judgment."

"You mean, like an interdimensional lawyer?"

"Perhaps, but a bit less biased. Those seeking our help or needing our judgment are tested with the scorpions. The venom in the scorpions helps you see the truth in the other person. In the end, if the person is guilty, the venom will take them under. Death is their punishment. If the judged is innocent, then you can heal them."

Tamara swallowed hard. "That seems a rather heavy burden to bear. What if the truth isn't clear?"

"You do not have to worry about that. If the truth is not clear, you have the choice of limited time travel to see the actions of the past. You will not be able to interfere with the actions, but you can view them and record notes," Serket explained.

"Why not use that method on every case?"

"Viewing the past can be traumatic. It can also allow you to see other things that may sway your decision. Therefore, I want vessels who are born leaders and problem solvers. You are more likely to make a calculated judgment based on all the evidence rather than a rash decision. You have already proven, even without magic, that you can make excellent decisions. That is, after all, why you are studying law, correct?"

Tamara smiled. Serket must have been watching her for a long time. She had never admitted to anyone that she was studying to become a lawyer because her parents despised them. In fact, she purposefully hid the prelaw degree behind a liberal arts major. Tamara had planned her whole career, from entry-level lawyer all the way to judgeship.

She wanted to help families like hers. When her father had been hurt in an accident, everyone had taken advantage of him. The insurance company, the lawyer, the judge—every single one of them had profited off her father's misfortune. Yet her father had been left with little financial stability and a permanent injury that prevented him from working. Her mother had had to go back to work at two different jobs to keep the family afloat.

Tamara was trying to get out of college early because one less year of tuition meant her mother could finally quit one of her jobs. As for law school, if she did well on her entrance exams, she would be in the running for several grants to pay for most of the expenses.

"Yes, I'm studying law in hopes of one day getting a judgeship."

Aella's mouth fell open. "You have no problem being a judge on Earth, but throw in a few magic scorpions and you balk at the chance?"

"I'm sorry. This whole vessel thing isn't part of my plan. I have a very structured timeline I must maintain. Being a judge for Serket was not something I ever considered. I'm sure you can both understand."

Serket nodded. "Yes, I do understand, but perhaps we can reach a compromise. May I grant you temporary abilities and allow you to perform a job for me right now so you can see what you would be doing? If you do not like it, I will release you and send you back to your home. I will even place you back on your birthday, prior to you receiving your mark. You will have lost no time in your life because of your visit here."

Tamara's mouth fell open in awe. "You can do that?"

"Yes, I can, for a short period, reverse time itself. Sometimes, I find I must for balance and order to be maintained. You are not the first initiate who did not want to stay."

Tamara twiddled her thumbs as she stood there, feeling Serket's eyes bearing down on her. What did she have to lose? By this time tomorrow, she'd be back in today, or something like that.

"How do I know what to do?"

"Come forth." Serket motioned Tamara nearer.

Tamara walked toward Serket and stopped in front of her. Serket touched her in the middle of her forehead and spoke a few words in a language Tamara couldn't decipher.

A tingle shot throughout Tamara's body as gusts of wind blew around her. The wind picked up the wisps of hair that had escaped her ponytail and whipped them around into her face. Something cold wrapped around her wrist. When she looked down, she saw a jeweled bracelet in the shape of a scorpion circling her forearm. A heavy weight pressed on her chest, and as she ran her hands over the area, she found a large metal necklace.

The magic bestowed on her coursed through Tamara's veins. It told her how to use the bracelet and the necklace to complete the task at hand. "Wow, this feels amazing. I feel so empowered. What is my assignment?"

"I am sending you back to the Earth dimension. It will be in your current time, but you will be sent to a small house in the state of Kentucky. When you knock on the door, you will want to ask for Alice. You will tell Alice that her whispers have been heard and you would like to come in to discuss the issues. From there, you will listen to her tale and act accordingly. Are you ready to try?"

Tamara nodded. "Yes, I am ready to meet Alice and try to help her."

Serket waved her hand, sending Tamara on her way.

Tamara appeared under a tree across the street from what she knew was Alice's house. The road was in a rather run-down neighborhood. The house before her was missing shingles, and a car sat on blocks in the yard. Looking down, Tamara was relieved to find herself dressed in blue jeans, a T-shirt, and a leather jacket. She didn't think the initiate outfit from the temple would have gone over well in this part of town. Taking a deep breath, Tamara crossed the street and knocked on the door.

The door opened, and a young woman about Tamara's age stood on the other side. A freckled face framed by bright red hair that hung down into hazel eyes peered back into Tamara's brown eyes. The woman scrunched her eyebrows and started to close the door. "We don't want nothing you're selling."

The statement threw Tamara off. She put her hand up on the door before it could close. "I'm not selling anything. I'm here to see Alice. Is she here?"

The woman stared at Tamara for a moment. "Are you a collections officer?"

"No, I'm here to tell Alice her whispers have been heard. I'm here to answer them."

The woman's eyes lit up. She grabbed Tamara's hand and pulled. "Come on in, please. I've been praying ever so hard for Serket to hear me."

"She's heard you, and she sent me. What's the problem you're having?"

Alice motioned toward the couch. It was stained and had giant holes in the fabric. "You'll want to sit down for this tale."

Tamara begrudgingly sat on the couch. She remembered what it was like the first year after her dad had gotten hurt. How they had had to sell all their nice furniture and move to a small apartment. Their new couch had come from a dumpster and looked much like this one. "All right, tell me everything."

"My dad died last year. Right now, it's just me and my older brother. He was trying to make some quick money and found out about a gig around town. He ended up running drugs for the local sheriff.

"Something went wrong with one of the deals, and my brother got shot. They couldn't call the cops to the scene, so they left Johnny there to bleed out and die. But the thing is, he didn't die. Somebody found him dragging himself down a back road and took him to the hospital. They patched him up and he was all right, but he wouldn't tell them how he got shot. The hospital called the sheriff, and the next thing I know, my brother is locked up with no chance of parole.

"I've been trying to get work in town, but nobody wants to hire me because of my brother. The sheriff wants Johnny to keep his mouth shut and take the fall, but he's afraid I'll get Johnny to talk. The sheriff's been trying to drive me out of town to keep me away from my brother and protect his fat ass. I know Johnny was breaking the law by carrying the weed, but it isn't fair that the sheriff gets to walk away while me and Johnny suffer.

"I don't have anywhere else to turn. Can you help me?"

Tamara's heart broke as she listened to Alice recount her tale. Wasn't this exactly the kind of situation she wanted to help with by becoming a judge in the first place? Plus, this poor woman would never be able to get help from the justice system. She was a case future Tamara wouldn't have been able to help with, but right now, as a vessel of Serket, she could.

"Yes, I'll help you get judgment passed on the sheriff. What is his name?"

"Patrick Linton. He hangs out at the sheriff's office during the day. Just go in and say you want to see him. Since you ain't a regular around here, he'll see you right away. Plus, it doesn't hurt none that you're pretty." Alice blushed.

Tamara stood and took her leave of Alice. She got directions for the station from the map app on her phone and walked the two blocks. Within fifteen minutes, she was entering the station. An older man sat at the front desk, asleep. Tamara walked up to the desk and cleared her throat.

The older man jumped a bit and almost fell out of his chair. He looked up to see Tamara watching him. "Yes, what do you want?"

"I would like to speak to Sheriff Linton, please."

The little man mashed the red intercom button. "Sheriff Linton, you have a guest at the front desk. Do you want me to send her on back?"

"Yes," replied a male voice through the intercom.

Tamara followed the directions the older man gave her for getting to the back of the building, where Sheriff Linton's office was located. When Tamara walked through an open door, she didn't immediately see anyone in the office. She was turning to make sure she had come the right way when the door shut in her face before she could leave. She looked to her left, and there, where the door had been covering the wall, stood a man. He was grinning from ear to ear and his fat belly hung out of his unbuttoned shirt.

"I was beginning to think Madame Jovia had run out of new guests to send me." The man walked closer to Tamara, sizing her up. He picked up a handful of her dark hair and inhaled, moaning softly.

Tamara spun away, removing her hair from his hands. "What in the world are you doing? I'm here to see Sheriff Linton."

The man grabbed Tamara and wrapped his arms around her waist. He planted a big kiss on her cheek. "I know you're here to see me. Are you that dense? All looks and no brains? Eh, I don't care. Get naked and lay on your back on my desk. You've been a very bad girl. I'm going to have to probe you for contraband."

Tamara, appalled, hauled off and hit the man with a right hook. "How about you keep your disgusting mouth shut? I'm not here for your pleasure."

Linton stumbled back, cupping his hands over his nose to catch the blood now oozing down his face. "You dumb brat! You're going to pay for that little outburst."

Before Linton could grab her again, Tamara touched her

scorpion bracelet. A million tiny scorpions sprang from the jeweled center and spread out to cover Linton. They drove their stingers into his soft flesh, sending him to the ground in a trance.

"Tell me, Sheriff Linton, did you have Johnny locked up to keep him quiet about your drug ring? Have you been trying to run his sister out of town?"

The scorpions receded and crawled back into Tamara's bracelet, leaving the stunned body of the sheriff on the office floor. In a rather odd voice, the man answered, "Why, yes. How did you know?"

"Magic, Sheriff Linton. I am magic. So, you admit Johnny did nothing so wrong as to be stuck in jail with no parole? And that Alice has been collateral damage of your greed?"

The fat lump on the floor moved a bit. "Yes, I forged the papers on Johnny and pinned the drug deal on him. The judge is in my pocket. He'll do as I say. Alice, I need her gone. She'll convince Johnny to talk. I can't have that. It's an election year."

Tamara walked over to the desk and grabbed a legal pad of paper and a pen. She walked back to the sheriff and threw the items down beside him. "I want you to write out a full confession and sign it."

Under her command, the man did as Tamara demanded. He wrote out his misdeeds of the last several years. He named names and listed a whole slew of innocent bystanders who'd been sent to jail in his attempt to cover up his own crimes. When he was done, he signed his name and handed the pages back to Tamara.

"Good, now I want you to call and have Johnny released from jail. Then I want you to summon the officer who distrusts you the most to come collect your confession."

Linton got up off the floor and walked over to the phone. He dialed Judge Harold's number. "Harold, it's Patrick. Look, I need to drop all the charges against Johnny. I got a better lead on who really did the crime. Yeah, I'm not joking. Go on and do it. Bye."

The sheriff absentmindedly pushed the intercom button. "Major Hoover, can you come in here please?"

Tamara hid behind the door and watched as a uniformed officer walked into the room. Astonishment broke out across the officer's face as he read the confession, and he ran out the door with it in his hands. Tamara was satisfied that Major Hoover would make sure arrest warrants were issued for the list of criminals, including Sheriff Linton.

Tamara smiled. "Good job, Sheriff Linton. You have really done a lot of good for this community. I think you deserve a special gift."

"Will you kill me now and release me from this hell you've put me through?"

It seemed Sheriff Linton was aware of the ramifications of his actions. Tamara smiled as she laid her hands on his shoulders. "That would be too much of a gift for you. I want to see you doing heavy labor."

Tamara's hands glowed bright green as she drew the poison out of his system. Patrick Linton sat motionless as tears rolled down his cheeks.

"What have you done to me?"

"I passed judgment on you. You were found lacking, and by your own hand, at that."

Tamara felt an odd tugging on her being, and then she reappeared in the Temple of Serket.

Serket sat on a golden throne, smiling. "Well, how was your trial job?"

Tamara couldn't hold back her excitement. "You knew I'd want to help the woman. This was both to prove I could do the job and to get me hooked on it, right?"

Serket nodded. "Yes, it was a test to prove you could do the job. I could explain it for centuries, but sometimes on-the-job training is a better explanation. Have you made your decision?"

"Yes, I want to accept your offer to be an angel of judgment and a vessel of Serket."

Serket rose from her throne and walked down to Tamara. She held out her hand and touched Tamara's forehead. She muttered more indecipherable words, and there was a flash of light.

"I'll return you to the day after you received your mark. You will be my agent in the Earth dimension. For your safety, you will only remember what you are when you are active in your duties. Otherwise, you will simply be the Tamara you've always been."

The words floated around in Tamara's head. She started to wake up and wondered what they meant. A tinge of anxiety caused Tamara's eyes to fly open. She sat up and took in her surroundings. No strange statues or cold caves greeted her; she was safe in her dorm room.

That had been some dream.

She looked at her alarm clock. The face showed that it was six o'clock on the morning of November 1. Tamara scooted to the edge of her bed to stretch. The movement caused a pounding in her head.

How many drinks did I have last night?

Feeling chilly, she rubbed the tops of her arms with her hands to get her blood circulating. When her hand brushed over the top of her right arm, a searing pain shot down to her hand. Expecting some sort of drunken injury, Tamara rose to look in the dresser mirror. Lifting her sleeve, she was surprised to find a medium-sized tattoo covering her upper arm and shoulder. It was a depiction of an ankh with a scorpion coming through the middle.

Where in the world did I get that?

ƀurneð Out

Amanda Mills Woodlee

atteo was perfect. Well, not really—he did chew his fingernails instead of cutting them—but he was the closest thing to it that Junie had found in sixteen years of dating. And at thirty-two years old, she was running out of options.

On paper, Junie was not the kind of woman one would think would be getting desperate. She was still on the right side of thirty-five, had an eternally twenty-six face and body, and supported herself with a solid job that had enabled her to buy her own home and create a nice cushiony savings account. She had everything.

But that was the problem, according to her dad.

"You're a wonderful girl," he assured her. "But you can be a bit, well, intimidating." He cast a nervous glance at Junie's mom.

Her mother insisted there was nothing wrong with that. "If they can't take a little heat, they don't belong in the kitchen." She eyed Junie's father, daring him to argue.

"I'm not saying you shouldn't be yourself, Junie-Bug," he cajoled. "Just maybe let 'em get to know you bit by bit. Then they'll love you like we do." He smiled and patted the back of her hand.

Junie tried. It wasn't hard to meet men in her line of work as it was a male-dominated field, but she didn't like the idea of dating anyone she worked with and most of them were married anyway. At the same time, always traveling made it hard to meet a guy at home.

And it wasn't as if Junie didn't want to find a guy. She did like the idea of having someone around, someone to go places with and do the whole family thing with. So one day, after she'd turned off the "Fasten Seatbelt" light, she switched on her phone, downloaded a dating app, and made a profile.

She filled it with things that were true: she did love animals, though frequent trips to Europe meant that keeping a pet alive was impossible; no guy wanted to know why a woman's betta fish was named Victim 14 or why she had labeled its tank The Swimming Dead. She left out the things that usually drove men away: her job, education, income, and fitness achievements. The profile picture she chose was flattering, but moreover, she looked approachable in it: her hair in loose waves, a demure smile that didn't show any teeth (*too aggressive,* she thought), and a flowy dress. She did crop it so her well-muscled calves didn't show.

It worked! By the time she touched down in Denver, she had several interested bachelors. She deleted the messages that were obviously from bots and replied to the rest of the flirtatious greetings with a simple "hi :)."

Through a series of equally vapid replies, she kept up conversations with a couple of potential "suitors." One, Brett, eventually suggested they meet for coffee. When Junie kept turning him down due to her flight schedule, he took it as her being coy and upped the ante to lunch. When Junie had to turn him down again, he messaged her, "*Chez Feu.* Saturday. 7. You can't say no to that." It worked out that Junie was off that day and the next, so she happily replied, "C u there. I'll be the one in green. ;)."

He beat her to the French restaurant, even though she was fifteen minutes early. After greeting her with a kiss on the cheek, he offered her his arm and guided her inside. When they were shown to their table in a private room, he insisted on pulling out her chair for her instead of allowing the server to do it. Then he instructed the man to bring them "the real champagne" and two glasses—flutes, not bird baths.

Junie was starting to think she could get used to this.

They made small talk while waiting for their server to return, keeping it light and flirty. Once their champagne had been poured, the server asked if they were ready to order. Junie started to tell him she would like the lamb, but Brett cut her off. In cringeworthy French, he asked if the chef could come up with something special for them. Junie understood it, despite the mess he made of his vowels and conjugation, because she'd spent several long vacations in France and had made a point of learning the language.

But the server, who Junie figured was probably a college student trying to afford both booze and books, apologized, saying that he didn't speak French at all. Brett sighed with over-the-top resignation and repeated his request in slow, enunciated English. When the server replied in the negative, Brett said, "Why don't you go check with him, just to be sure." The server glanced at Junie, who gave him a subtle, empathetic shrug, before deciding to comply.

Brett adjusted his napkin in his lap. "My apologies, June. I used to come here all the time; the sea bass was exquisite. Seems they must have changed management since I was last here. You never would have even been allowed to order in English before."

Junie gave him a tight smile. She had the distinct feeling she was not going to be gushing to her friends about this date after all.

When the server returned and, apologizing, informed them that the chef indeed did not have any specials that evening, Junie jumped in. "You know, that lamb really did look good. I'd like that." She handed him the menu.

Brett sniffed. "Well, I guess I'll have the sea bass."

The server apologized again, explained that that item was not currently on the menu.

Brett closed his eyes, appearing to collect himself. "Exactly what *do* you have?"

The server recommended the coq au vin.

"I didn't come here to eat *chicken*. What else?"

Junie shifted in her seat. The server suggested the bouillabaisse.

"Soup? Really? Wow. Just tell the chef to impress me. If he can."

When the server scuttled away—no doubt to eviscerate Brett with his coworkers—Brett said to Junie, "I'm sorry. We can still go elsewhere if you'd like."

Junie insisted she'd rather stay, restraining herself from adding, "But you can go, if you'd like." This evening would be over soon enough. May as well eat and stick around for the rest of The Brett Show. She downed half her champagne in one swallow.

"So, June, your profile said you work at an airport, was that right?"

"In a way. I work in the airline industry."

"Interesting," he said without seeming to hear her. "What are you, a stewardess?"

Something must've flickered in her eyes at that, some irritation she had betrayed, because he added quickly, "Or what is it you like to be called now—flight attendants, right?" His conciliatory smile oozed condescension. "Sorry, old habit. I practically lived at airports for my first job."

Junie set her drink down with precise movements. *Keep your cool, Junie. This is not the first time you've heard this.*

"Yes, they do prefer that," she replied in measured tones. When he looked somewhat relieved, she considered allowing the mistaken notion of her occupation but decided that sort of deception was too much effort to be worth it. Might as well see where the truth took her. "But I'm not a flight attendant. Actually, I'm a pilot."

That got his attention. He gave a laugh, clearly thinking she was cracking a joke. She held his gaze until he realized she was serious.

He fumbled for a way to recover and apparently went with the first straw he could get hold of. "Sorry, I just didn't know there were any . . . lady pilots."

The words *lady pilots* clanged like an echoing gong in Junie's head. Her chest grew hot, and her breathing quickened. She closed her eyes and tried to slow it back down. The date might have been awful, but she didn't need to make it worse.

Junie picked up her glass again and drained it before answering. With as much control as she could muster, she said, "Yes, there are *lady* pilots. Just like there are *lady* doctors and *lady* lawyers." Then she smiled—with all her teeth—and added, "Who knew?"

Brett tried to recover. "Well, that's great. I mean, good for the girls, right?" He began talking haltingly about how much he supported women and how he had taken home ec in high school, swearing that it wasn't just so he could meet girls, though he admitted he did date several of his classmates.

All in all, Junie was relieved when the entrées arrived. She was fully prepared to shovel her food like she was being timed. If she threw it up all over him, it would be the perfect excuse to leave quickly. Maybe snap a selfie first: a memory to treasure always.

The server set a beautiful plate of lamb lollipops down in front of her. Then Junie watched as he set before Brett a dish of what appeared to be duck confit, which she could only hope had been basted with large quantities of spit from some preferably ill kitchen cooks with current flare-ups of herpes.

"What's this?" Brett demanded.

The server confirmed Junie's guess and elaborated.

"I know what duck confit is. What I'm wondering is why it's in front of me. I said surprise me, and this is what he goes with?"

The server blinked, obviously at a loss.

Junie jumped in. "Well, you're surprised, aren't you?"

The server let a bark of laughter escape before he clamped his mouth shut, but it was too late. Brett began to fume. He stood up and threw his napkin on the floor. He stared the server down.

"C'mon, June. This place has gone to the dogs. We'll find someplace else with better service."

Junie eyed her lamb hungrily. "I'm fine here, thank you."

Brett looked at her. "I said, let's go." He turned on the server and began poking him in the chest. "You will never work in a restaurant again, and I'll see to it that this place is shut down before you can even collect your next paycheck. You made a big mistake tonight, a *big*—"

Before he could finish the sentence, Brett was gone. Not "gone" as in out the door. "Gone" as in out of this life. Dead. Expired. History. He was like warmed bread: toast.

In his place was a pile of grayish-white ashes, out of which stuck the molten form of a wristwatch.

Junie coughed around the warm feeling in her throat.

Oops.

It wasn't the first time this had happened. She had had to move for her senior year of high school, when she was the last person to be seen with Joey Barushki before he disappeared. The police could only come to a girl's door so many times before her fellow students started putting space between her and them.

Unlike the unfortunate Brett, though, Joey had been an accident. Mostly, anyway. She hadn't known of her power then, but she had meant to send him a strong message when he groped her on a date in the woods. Fortunately, her parents told the police she'd been home all weekend with a sore throat—true enough—and with no physical evidence to support their suspicions, they'd been forced to cease interrogating her. It had helped that her mom was a lawyer who was scary enough in her own rights.

In exchange for the alibi, her parents had demanded the truth. Junie had feared they would lock her up in a psychiatric ward when she told them, but her mom's face didn't budge a millimeter as Junie related how she had burned Joey to a crisp and arranged the ashes to look like part of a campfire. Joey's molten keys, which had never been recovered, she'd tossed in the deep waters of the nearby blue hole they had originally trekked in to see.

"I thought it might be something like that," her mom had said when Junie was done. In reply to Junie's quirked eyebrow, she added, "You get it from me."

And that was all the explanation Junie ever got.

She had had some near misses since then, but she'd managed to keep a tight rein on her anger. It helped that she had avoided dating altogether. When going to a bar with a guy might end with her *behind bars*, Junie tended to decide the risk wasn't worth it.

But now she really wanted that whole white-picket-fence scene. Her friends flooded her social media with pictures of their weddings and precious families. Junie had begun to wonder if she'd ever have her turn.

Now Junie was wondering how strong the pen pal system would be at the prison she was likely headed for. She looked at the server, whom she now thought of as Witness A. He was staring at the ash heap on the marble floor. After a minute of listening to her heart beating in her ears, Junie watched as he turned to look at her at last. She had her mouth open to explain when he spoke in a small but even voice.

"Would you like the check now?"

Junie nodded.

Once he had returned with the bill, he mechanically packed all the food in to-go containers. She pulled out a substantial stack of cash from her purse and laid it on the receipt without even looking at the amount. Then he handed her the boxes, which he had placed in a paper bag.

"My compliments to the chef. . . . Will that be enough?" she asked as she accepted them and gave him the money.

"Plenty," he answered without even looking. "And she thanks you, I'm sure." He bade her a pleasant evening.

After that, Junie never went anywhere without a large stash of cash, her passport, and a change of clothes, including a hat.

She wondered how long it would be before the police came to question her, and she spent every hour she was on land looking over her shoulder. Flying became the only time she could get some peace. A constant hum of panic gripped her for the first few weeks. After an entire season had passed without so much as a single officer knocking on her door, Junie finally started to relax.

Then she met Matteo, and things started looking up. They were having drinks side by side in a Parisian airport lounge when he leaned over and, in decent French, told her she looked familiar. She thought about accusing him of using a lame pickup line, but he looked familiar to her too.

"Did you just get in on flight 280?"

"I did!" He sounded surprised—and a little relieved, probably because she had replied in English.

"Then you saw my face when you boarded."

He took a moment to process this, then snapped his fingers as it clicked. "The pilot! Got it. Didn't recognize you out of uniform. Well, shoot," he bemoaned. "The next question is usually 'So what do you do for a living?' and here I already know the answer, so now I don't know what to say to keep you talking to me."

He smiled so disarmingly when he said this that Junie couldn't help smiling back at him.

"You could tell me what you do for a living," she suggested.

"I could, but it's not nearly interesting enough to keep the conversation going."

Junie laughed at his self-deprecation. "Being a pilot isn't all that interesting, either. All I do is go back and forth between airports— I'm a taxi driver with wings. Whatever you do is bound to be more fascinating."

He stuck his hand out at her. "I'm Matteo."

She took his proffered hand. "Junie."

They conversed in this light way for a couple of hours, and for the first time in months, Junie found herself having a good time on the ground. Even better, it turned out Matteo lived less than an hour from her back in the States.

She had arranged her schedule so she could stay in Paris for the week, hoping it might rejuvenate her. Matteo said he was an investor in France on vacation, so they wound up spending most of the week together. When the happy week sadly came to a close, he shyly asked if he could continue seeing her "in the real world," and she agreed.

He didn't play it cool when they got back, either. By the time she landed, she had a voicemail from him asking her to dinner. Not a text, an actual call. She immediately called him back and told him she'd love to.

Now, they'd been dating a few weeks, and he was asking if she was ever going to introduce him to her parents. She agreed to ask them about it and would have left the plans undefined, but he pressed her about it again the next day. With open enthusiasm, her parents invited them to dinner at their house that same weekend.

So that was how Junie and Matteo found themselves trudging up her parents' driveway on Sunday evening, hand in hand. Junie was sure she was more nervous than Matteo. She could tell he was agitated, but it seemed to be more from excitement than fear.

Her dad was all smiles; Junie couldn't remember ever seeing him so happy. When they were introduced, he shook Matteo's hand until Junie thought he might pull Matteo's arm out of its socket. He laughed too readily and loudly at anything Matteo said. And Junie could have sworn he started to choke up when he said, "We're just thrilled that our little Junie's finally found a feller."

With a significant look at her husband, Junie's mom took that opportunity to ask Matteo if he'd care for a glass of wine or spirits.

"I wouldn't turn down a glass of whatever was handed to me," he replied in a friendly manner. "While you pour, how about I have Junie give me a tour of the place where she grew up?"

"I think that's a splendid idea," her mother said. "Junie, just bring him to the back deck when you're done." Then she ushered her reluctant husband into the kitchen.

"I'm sorry about my dad," Junie said on their way up the stairs. "He's just a little excited, is all. I've never brought a guy home before."

"That's understandable—that he'd be excited, I mean. Not that you've never brought a guy home. That's surprising."

Junie declined to go down that line of conversation. They reached her bedroom first, and she opened the door and flicked on the lights to reveal a sparsely decorated room.

"Guest bedroom?" Matteo guessed.

"My bedroom," Junie corrected.

"I take it your minimalist phase hit early?" he asked teasingly.

Junie laughed softly. "We moved here for my senior year of high school. I didn't have much time to decorate before I graduated and went to college."

"Yikes! Moved senior year? That had to have been rough."

Junie shuffled her feet. "It was a relief, actually."

"Ah. Had some trouble with your classmates, I take it?"

"You could say that."

He stepped to her side, wrapped his arm around her, and kissed her temple. After a moment, he said, "Where are your yearbooks? We'll find the ones who bothered you and make fun of them together." His grin made Junie laugh, despite the old feelings that being here had stirred up. He espied her bookshelf and found her yearbooks. "Where's your junior year?"

"I didn't get that one."

He grabbed her sophomore yearbook instead. "This will have to do, then." He flipped through and found her class. "All right, which one of these clowns gave you trouble? I'll teach them not to pick on my Junie-Bug."

Junie pointed to her own picture.

"What?" he asked disbelievingly. "This adorable creature? She wouldn't bother anyone. Look at those eyes. That's the kind of face that spends Friday nights playing checkers with lecherous men at old folks' homes. C'mon, tell me, or I'll be forced to guess. How about this girl? That's a bully if ever I saw one. You can hardly blame her, though. Probably had to learn to be tough with a last name like that. Geez, did no one tell her ancestors that vowels were free?"

Junie laughed in spite of herself. Matteo was just reaching his stride, though. "Not her? What about this guy? I think if he had another brain cell, he'd have to buy new hats."

Junie was in stitches and begging him to leave off, but he flipped a couple of pages, to the class ahead of hers. "Oh, I got it. What about this guy? Looks like a real Don Juan." He pushed the picture of Joey under her nose, and her laughter died in an instant.

"We should go meet my parents downstairs." She turned toward the door.

Matteo reached for her hand and pulled her back. "Hey," he said in a soothing voice. "I'm sorry. I obviously hit a nerve . . . maybe you should talk about it, whatever it was."

"It was nothing. He was just a kid who . . . disappeared the next year."

Matteo rubbed his thumb across the back of her hand. "And you liked him?"

Junie's eyes flashed. "No."

"Ah. So you hated him?"

She didn't answer.

"Did you have something to do with his death?"

She went still.

"I never said he died."

Matteo fumbled for a moment. "Well, I just assumed . . . after all these years . . ."

Junie faced Matteo fully. "How did we get to talking about Joey Barushki?" When he squirmed but didn't answer, she pressed for more. "Where are you from? Where did you go to school? Did you know Joey?"

Matteo looked like he was making up his mind about something. Finally, in a small voice, he admitted, "I might have gone to a nearby school and heard some rumors."

The earth shifted beneath her.

"Junie, I would never tell anyone."

She began backing away from him. She could feel the anger rising like magma inside her. Her blood roared through her ears. Matteo followed her, making appeasing motions with his hands.

"Truly," he continued. "I knew enough about Joey to know he

probably deserved worse than whatever he got. He took my cousin on a date once, and she was never the same after that."

"But how can I possibly trust you, knowing you kept this from me?"

"You just gotta, Junie. That's what love's about: trust."

Her chest cooled a little. After all, would he have willingly been in a relationship with her if he was going to tell anyone? Unless . . .

"Are you recording this? Because you know it can't be used as evidence."

He held up his hands to show his palms before he emptied his pockets and showed her their insides. Her still-icy stare prompted him to begin unbuttoning his dress shirt.

"You know, if your parents come up here with me like this, they might have some questions." He gave her a devilish smile.

"Just finish stripping."

He did. After kicking off his pants and boxer briefs, he spun a slow 360-degree turn to complete the examination.

"Satisfied?" he asked, an eyebrow arched suggestively.

Junie ignored the heat of a different kind that she was beginning to feel. "What do you want?"

"Isn't it obvious?"

She rolled her eyes impatiently. "Enough flirting. Out with the truth."

He sobered a little. Holding up his hands again, he reached slowly for a nearby jar candle. He gestured for her to observe, so she watched as he breathed lightly and lit the wick. Junie stared at the dancing flame, which didn't look like normal fire or her fire; it was a cool blue, where hers was red orange.

He spoke in a mesmerizing tone. "I want what you want: to see the bad people go bye-bye. To purge the world of the Joey Barushkis and the Kim Schraeders."

"Who's she?"

His face twisted a little. "Let's just say she's my Joey. My first one, anyway."

"There've been others?"

He made a considering face. "There might've been a few." He let this sink in before going on. "Think of what we could do together. Joey never would have seen the inside of a jail, even if you had gone to the police. You know that. We can make sure that justice is served."

Junie shook her head confusedly. "You're talking about murder."

"Murdering bad people."

"But who are we to tell who's bad?"

"Was Joey bad, hm?"

"That was different!" Junie insisted. "I didn't know what would happen then."

"Are you telling me Joey's the only one, then?" He eyed her skeptically. "There's more than one Kim. I'm betting there's more than one Joey."

Junie couldn't deny that. Brett hadn't been an accident the same way Joey had. Sure, Brett had been a grade-A jerk, but she'd only *kind of* meant to turn him into cinders; she'd really just lost control. And afterward, she'd felt awful.

She shook her head. "I don't want to do that. I never meant to hurt anyone. I'm sorry, Matteo."

He looked at her with obvious disappointment. "Are you sure, really?"

She nodded solemnly.

Matteo sighed and handed her the jar candle, which she kept her eyes trained on while he dressed. While he buckled his belt, he asked one more time. When she repeated her no, he said, "I hate to do it this way, but you know I could twist your arm a bit. I know things. I know your parents know. Your mom's a lawyer, right? Dad's got a good job. What would happen if someone suggested they lied during an investigation?"

Junie looked at him as if it were the first time she'd ever seen him. The half smile she'd found charming before suddenly resembled Joey's cocky grin.

"Tell you what," he added, making his way for the door. "How about I let you sleep on it? You can let me know tomorrow." He twisted the handle of the door and began to pull it open.

"Wait, Matteo . . ."

Junie's dad entered the bedroom carrying an extra glass of wine. He looked around the room, his smile falling slowly. Then he turned his eyes on Junie, who was setting down a jar candle. "What happened to your feller?"

"He had to go."

My Pukis

D. Marie Prokop

Wisconsin, USA, summer 1975

om's basketball-shaped belly brushed the steering wheel as she exited the new station wagon.

Already out of the car, I spied my grandmother from the driveway. "Oma!"

"Beth! How I've missed you," she said. A smile creased the edges of her rosy face.

It was a sunny June day, one week after school had let out. We had arrived at Oma's home in the Wisconsin Dells an hour behind schedule because Mom stopped to use the bathroom at the fast food place, the gas station, and three interstate rest stops.

My world would change after the baby came. Probably for the worse. Mom was difficult enough to deal with. Soon, I'd also have a whining baby brother or sister to contend with.

When Mom was in a good mood, she spoiled me. On those days, my best friend, Susie, was jealous. Her parents wouldn't let her do anything—eat sugary cereals, watch television, or wear bell-bottoms. It was awful. We never stayed overnight at her place. So when Mom was happy, Susie slept over at our house. Mom let us do whatever we wanted. We usually camped out in the living room, stayed up late watching movies, and ate popcorn and candy bars until our stomachs hurt.

Those were the good times—the happy Mom days. The rest of the time, my mother—well—she was a monster. My stepdad, Ronnie, called her princess and obeyed her every command. He was the only one who could calm Mom down when the unhappy monster inside her reared its head. If the mailman was late, the bill too high, the service too slow, the weather too cold, or my room too messy, Mom had a fit. Ronnie would rub her neck, kiss her cheek, and whisper magic words into her ear. She'd sigh like a resigned queen reigning over her pitiful subjects and retreat to her room. Ronnie's magic had saved me from her wrath more than once.

This pregnancy had been a whirlwind of fits and calm. Spending the summer with Oma was just what I needed. No more walking on eggshells or frantic telephone calls to Ronnie's office to tame Mom's temper.

When we walked into Oma's house, familiar smells of boiled cabbage, stale mothballs, and wool greeted me.

The house looked different, though. Instead of avocado-green paint, pink wallpaper with tiny red flowers and blue stripes adorned the walls of the living room. New thick white carpet curled around my sneakers.

"Interesting," Mom commented, her sharp blue eyes taking in the new decor.

Oma folded a white crocheted blanket, matching the corners, and smoothed it over the back of an armchair. Mom's vague comment might have rattled most people, but my grandmother stayed composed. She'd known her—and her moods—the longest.

Mom began critiquing the "old-fashioned" wallpaper as I ran to retrieve my luggage. By the time I returned with my suitcase and stuffed dragon, my mother's criticism had shifted from the walls to the furniture. "That vintage cedar chest clashes with everything. You should keep it in the basement."

Flames flashed in Oma's dark eyes, and for a second, I thought she might raise her voice. Instead, she inhaled deeply, slow as a tortoise, and lowered her chin. "You're right, of course. Beth can help me move it this summer."

Mom embraced me quickly and warned me not to give Oma any trouble or I would have to answer to her. "By the time you come home, you'll have a new little brother or sister." She smirked, as if she relished causing me discomfort.

I smirked back. "Oh, joy," I mumbled. She frowned at me, but I closed the door on her disapproval.

Turning my back to the door, I smiled widely at my tiny grandmother. "I think the chest is perfect right where it is, Oma." I wrinkled my brow. "Why haven't I seen it before? It looks old."

Sadness crept into the corners of her thin smile. "Oh, I wanted it to be a surprise. It's a gift for you. For your future."

"For me? Thank you, Oma!" I hugged her small frame. I'd been much shorter than her last summer. I'd only grown an inch this year. Maybe she'd shrunk. Old people did that, I'd heard.

I tried to imagine Oma as a twelve-year-old girl like me, but I couldn't do it.

Oma bent over and opened the chest. The powerful perfume of cedar filled my nostrils. It almost choked me. Though I prefer the smell of cedar over the disgusting aroma of mothballs, I pinched my nose before I leaned over and peered into the chest.

A kaleidoscope of colorful wool items filled the smelly cavity. Oma relaxed on the floor, lowering her petite frame onto the shaggy carpet. She patted one hand on the white fluff, inviting me to get comfortable beside her, so I did.

She lifted an item from the chest: a mitten unlike any other mitten. A blue-and-white scalloped design, like foamy waves cresting the shore, edged the cuff. Stripes of yellow and green separated the cuff from the hand. Colorful patterns, more intricate than Oma's new wallpaper, filled the remainder.

"Did you knit this?" I asked.

Oma nodded, showing me its match, then folded the pair and placed it gingerly back into the chest. Eager to see more, I couldn't stop myself from reaching in and grasping the most intriguing knitwear I'd ever seen—a soft black-and-white pair with fringed edges and geometric patterns throughout. The mittens were complex in their simplicity.

"I like this." I traced a thick cord resembling a black-and-white zipper.

Oma's smile reached her dark eyes, brightening them to a warm brown. "Ah, the Latvian braid. It's a technique I learned when I was your age. The strands of yarn twist around each other in the first step. If you perform the second step correctly, they untwist. It's magical."

"It sounds difficult. I can't believe you made all these. How many are there?"

Oma sighed and shrugged her small shoulders. "I don't know. I lost count. They're yours now. When you get married, you and your husband can count them. Promise you'll remember me when you do."

Husband? Good grief, Oma. "I will."

An ache filled my heart. These mittens were Oma's, not mine. I couldn't take them from her. But Oma put her cool, soft hand over my mouth before I could protest.

"It's tradition. Your mother refused this dowry chest, but I will go to my grave a content woman knowing they will be in your possession one day. Promise me." Her face flushed a deep pink.

I nodded. The tears falling down Oma's cheeks stung my heart.

As we examined the contents of the chest together, she regaled me with stories of her childhood. Oma had lived in a little town near Rīga, the capital city of Latvia, close to the Baltic Sea and "not far enough" from Russia.

"My elder sister was the most celebrated knitter in our community. Everything Liesma made was perfect—no mistakes allowed. She taught me to knit. Liesma was a harsh teacher, but I wanted the respect of the rest of the ladies in the village, so I obeyed. I made many mistakes at the beginning, but I learned. Oh, how I learned!"

When our stomachs both grumbled, Oma closed the chest. Her knees creaked as she rose.

"Beth, you haven't unpacked yet. Go to your room and organize your things while I make you some bread soup. When you're done, it'll be ready."

I nodded and grabbed my suitcases. In the darkness of the hall, I grimaced. Bread soup was not my favorite. But Oma had just told me how bread soup had been her favorite—until the Red Army invaded Latvia and bread became a luxury, then a memory.

Oma had been an adult in 1941, when she and my mom, then two years old, left their homeland during "The Horrible Year," as Oma called it. They had escaped to Finland. Eventually, they immigrated to the United States and settled here in Wisconsin. Oma married a literature professor with a heart condition. He died before I was born.

I tried to imagine Oma as a pretty young bride. My brain couldn't do it. Oma was Oma, making me her favorite childhood dish, gifting me her dowry chest, and telling me stories of the old days—good and bad.

I shut my eyes and tried to imagine myself as a grandmother. What foods would I make my grandchild? Popcorn? Groovy.

My room remained the same as I had left it last summer. Pastel pink walls and white lacy curtains. A small clock sat on top of the side table. Last year, Oma had put a television—the only color set in the house—in my room. The sheets smelled different from my ones at home, which had a perfumed, burnt odor. Mom enjoyed the convenience of the new dryer she'd begged Ronnie for, but Oma hung her laundry outside, except in the winter.

I unpacked, filled the empty dresser with my clothes, and placed my stuffed dragon on the quilt. Oma had given him to me last Christmas, but he still didn't have a name. My summer reading assignment was *The Once and Future King*. Since Merlin was my favorite character so far, I considered naming my dragon after the famous wizard.

After supper, I cleared the table. When I had finished, I found Oma sitting in her armchair, the white crocheted blanket draped over her legs like a fresh layer of snow. She pulled a bag from her basket and began knitting, holding the yarn and needles close to her eyes. My favorite television show came on soon, so I gave Oma a quick kiss on the cheek and rushed off.

Once the show had ended, I wandered to the kitchen for a glass of water. The living room was dark except for the lamp beside Oma's chair.

Oma slept soundly under the soft lamplight. Four metal needles, like short bicycle spokes, rested in her still hands. Two strands of wool—one black and one white—lay twisted across her snowy lap blanket and wound together into the basket below. The Latvian braid. Step one.

I tiptoed to the kitchen, trying not to wake Oma, and filled a glass with water from the faucet. My bare feet floated silently over the shag carpet; still, I walked slow and steady so my water wouldn't spill. From the corner of my eye, the cedar chest called to me. There were so many mittens inside I hadn't seen yet.

Sipping my water, I walked toward the chest. I set the glass on the floor, then lifted the lid. The hinges creaked like Oma's knees. Carefully, I removed the mittens—my mittens—setting the ones I'd already seen on the floor.

The mittens grew familiar to me, like my well-worn sneakers or my favorite comfy sweatshirt. I knew them. The blue-and-red pair with yellow on the cuff and thumb. The ones with a green-and-yellow geometric design and a white scalloped edge. And my favorite: the black-and-white fringed pair.

I held up the black-and-white beauties. They were longer than my hand. I yearned to put them on but wondered if it was bad luck to wear them before I got married. *I should ask Oma.* But I didn't have the heart to wake her. She slept peacefully in her chair with her knitting on her lap.

I separated the two mittens and deciphered which one was the left one. As I pulled the fabric over my hand, it warmed instantly. Pulling its match over my right hand, I noticed a hole on the palm.

The fabric wasn't cut or moth-eaten, but singed. Dingy gray edged the unfortunate wound.

"Beth?"

I gasped. Oma stood behind me, her hand on my shoulder.

"Sorry to frighten you, dear. What are you doing?"

I showed Oma the hole in the black-and-white mitten. Her countenance fell. That same sadness I'd noticed earlier, when she gifted me the dowry chest, returned.

"I didn't do it, Oma," I said.

Her thin lips pursed together. She took the mittens and examined the hole.

"I know, Beth. It wasn't you; it was a *pukís*."

"What's a *pukís*?" I asked, rising to my feet.

Oma's eyes darkened. "A dragon. A revered fire-breathing creature from my homeland. It did this."

"Uh, okay . . ."

Oma must have been getting a little batty. She'd never talked like this before. Sure, she had gifted me a stuffed dragon for Christmas, but she had never talked about dragons as if they were real or called them by their Latvian name.

Oma's mouth pulled into a half smile. "I'm not crazy, Beth. Let me tell you the story of how this mitten was burned. Then you'll understand."

I retrieved my glass of water and relaxed on the sofa across from Oma's armchair. Sitting, she placed her knitting back in the basket and smoothed the blanket across her legs. Grasping the black-and-white mittens in her hand, she began her story.

"It all started with a bicycle." Oma sighed. "Latvia had been occupied by Russia for years, but the Upitis family had lived unnoticed by Russia's secret police, the NKVD, until the stolen bicycle incident."

I pictured my new bike with the glittery, pink banana seat. It would have broken my heart if anyone had taken it from me. A bike was freedom.

"It was 1941. My sister, Liesma, was a young wife, mother, and master knitter. In Latvia, skilled artisans are highly valued. They keep our traditions, our history, and our way of life alive."

I'd heard about the value of Latvian artistry all my life, but after seeing the beautiful mittens, I finally understood why this skill was so admired. Mom scoffed at most old-fashioned things, but even she would never insult Latvian knitting. She respected the years of practice and dedication involved. Like Olympic athletes, Latvian knitters were the best of the best.

"Liesma's husband, Filips, owned a tailor shop. Every day, he rode to work on the family's bicycle. In the snow, in the rain, it didn't matter. One day, a Russian soldier 'borrowed' the bicycle."

"Then what happened? He wouldn't give it back?"

Oma scrunched her thin mouth and tsked. "He claimed it was his. Liesma was indignant. She visited the soldier's commanding officer and demanded the bicycle be returned. The officer dragged the thief into his office."

I leaned forward. "Did he make the soldier return the bicycle?"

Oma frowned. "Yes, but then he shot the soldier and declared that Filips would take the thief's place in the Red Army. Liesma was very, *very* angry."

"I bet." It was wrong to force a civilian to join the military, let alone fight for the enemy. That was worse than the draft.

"That Russian officer was a monster, a snake. But he was a tiny pest compared to my sister. Liesma was a *pukis*."

"A dragon? You don't mean for real? You mean she was *like* a dragon. Right?"

Oma shook her head. Her dark eyes flashed with a red light.

"The next day, the NKVD came. They captured Filips and claimed his property. 'This is Russia's house now,' they said. Liesma had the biggest collection of mittens in the entire district. She had three chests full."

My heart thudded against my ribcage. "Forget the mittens! What happened? Did they take Filips? Did they hurt Liesma?"

Oma's eyes studied the floor. She raised them, clenching her small jaw. "I was also there when the soldiers came. Liesma handed me her infant daughter and sent me away. 'Run into the forest and don't come back!' she said. I obeyed. The rest of the tale was told to me afterward by Liesma's neighbors." Oma grasped the burnt mitten in her lap. She sighed. "A whole company of Red Army soldiers forced their way into the house. A sudden explosion set the building on fire. None of the soldiers came out."

"And Liesma and Filips?"

Oma's face held a tortured look. "The neighbors only found this." She caressed the mitten. "They hid me and Liesma's baby until we could escape. They believed the fire was caused by a stray grenade, mishandled by the inexperienced young soldiers—some of them as young as you, sons of farmers—but I know the truth."

I still doubted. It was impossible. Dragons were the stuff of fiction, of fairy tales, of myth. There was no way Oma's sister had turned into a dragon and fought the Red Army in 1941.

Oma sighed. "You must think I'm a loony old woman. Maybe I am. But once, I had a sister who demanded respect and admiration. If she felt insulted, she turned on you." Oma pulled up her long sleeves. Scars marred her pink skin. Long scratch marks.

"Your sister did that?"

Oma nodded. "She was a *pukís*. I didn't learn how to handle her until I was about your age. I pleased her as well as I could."

My head swam. Liesma sounded like Mom. Before Ronnie came along and used his comfort magic on her, she had been a beast to live with, unpredictable, with an uncontrollable, fiery temper. Summer vacations with Oma had been the only times in my life when I could breathe easy, where I felt comfortable.

"Wait—you said Liesma sent you out of the house with her baby. What happened to the child?"

"I took her with me to Finland, then to the States."

"Do you mean—Mom is your niece, not your daughter? Does she know?"

Oma shook her head. The gray streaks in her hair glistened in the lamplight. Her wrinkled face—a frail, gentle version of my strong, stubborn mother's—glowed.

"Your mother knows what she wants to know. She had to be raised by someone who understood what she was. I couldn't give her up. She needed me. You need me too."

"Oma, am I a *pukis*?"

She chuckled. "No, Beth. Thank goodness. *Pukis* are rare, the servants of those who can control them. They are powerful, fickle beasts, but they protect their masters."

"Who's Mom's master?"

Oma's brow furrowed. "*You* are, Beth."

I scowl. "No way. I can't control her. Only Ronnie can."

Oma winked and patted my shoulder. "You will learn. And when you need protection, she will fight for you. Mothers protect their children. It's instinctual, especially for a *pukis*."

That night, I dreamed of dragons; Merlin was there, as well as the Red Army. A house was consumed by flames. A dragon leaped from the roof, holding a tiny baby in its mouth, and flew through rings of smoke into the black sky.

Latvia, spring 1992—16 years later

The international airport in Rīga was clean and plain, the gray floors polished to an impressive shine. Through the frosted windows, I spied patches of snow clinging to the green grass outside. I held my daughter's hand as we made our way to the baggage carousel.

After decades of occupation, Latvia had gained its independence last year, half a century after "The Horrible Year," when Liesma disappeared and Oma escaped to Finland with my mother.

The small airport bustled with people. Both businessmen and

families had spilled out of our plane. My three-year-old daughter, Zinta, dropped her stuffed dragon on the shiny airport floor.

"Liesma!" she cried. I halted so she could retrieve it. She grasped the ragged *pukís* by its wing.

Mom and Ronnie Jr. went on ahead. "I'll grab the bags, Sis," Ronnie declared.

I smiled at him. Strong as he was kind, my baby brother carried our suitcases into the brisk outdoors.

Oma had taught me to speak her native tongue before cancer stole her voice. Thankfully, my rusty language skills sufficed to procure us a taxi. We arrived safely at our hotel, a tall building with an impressive view of the city's skyline: white spires and gray rectangles poised against a background of steel-blue water, a matching sky, and ivory clouds.

The next morning, we prepared to venture outside. I pulled on a pair of mittens, a simple black-and-white pair I had knit myself after years of practice and correction from Oma. *No mistakes!* I'd kept my promise and thought of her every time I wore them. I remembered the flame in her dark eyes, her generosity and wisdom . . . and the *pukís*.

Mom grasped my arm. "What if she's poor or sickly—or a hunchback?" Mom was being Mom: self-centered, fierce, and temperamental. But I knew what to do with her now.

"Oh, I'm sure she's just as beautiful as you are. Surely you inherited your fabulous good looks from her." Mom's eyes lit up. Compliments were her food. She gobbled them right up. It worked like magic.

Before Oma—Zinta Anderson—passed on, she had hired an investigator to search for her long-lost sister, Liesma, in the belief she had lived and escaped Latvia. A month ago, the investigator had found a widow who fit the description Oma had provided, an expatriate who'd recently returned to Rīga.

We had arranged to meet Mom's birth mother at a quiet café near the Daugava River. I handed our taxi driver a paper with the address. He dropped us off at an intersection a block away. "Is hard to park," he explained in English, then sped away, black smoke billowing from the tailpipe of the rusted boxy sedan.

We started walking toward the café. A group of teenagers, mostly boys, elbowed each other as we passed and spoke unfamiliar phrases. Ignoring their comments, we kept our heads down and continued walking.

They jumped off their perches along the wall and followed us. Before we could reach the end of the block, the group had formed a circle around us and slowed to a stop, blocking our path. I squeezed Zinta tightly to my chest and grasped my brother's coat sleeve.

Ronnie patted my hand. "They're just hungry orphans. They probably want a handout." He tossed some coins at the scrawny teenagers surrounding us.

I pleaded with them in Latvian. "Please, take this money and go."

They laughed as they swept up the coins and stuffed them into their coat pockets.

I could sense Mom's temper rising. "What do you hoodlums want? Go away!" she yelled. The air around her warmed.

Chastisement in English from an angry lady did nothing to assuage their delinquent minds. If anything, she'd antagonized them.

They danced around us, linked at the elbows. Their cold expressions lacked sympathy. Beady eyes bore into us, hungry and desperate.

They spoke stilted English. "Tourists? American pigs?" they teased, poking at our clothes and guffawing. "Rich folks, huh? You have more money. Give us more. Give us your coats!"

One of the ruffians tugged hard at Mom's jacket from behind, ripping the lapel. She elbowed him in the stomach. He growled, spun her around, and slapped her across the face. Ronnie stepped between them and shoved the boy down. The teen pulled out a switchblade and pointed it at him.

I clasped Zinta tighter in my arms. She cried for her stuffed dragon, which once again lay on the ground. "Liesma! Liesma!"

An elderly woman pushing a walker appeared from around the corner. Hearing her name, my biological grandmother replied in Latvian, "Daughter? I'm here."

The gang charged her. When they knocked the walker out of her hands, she crumpled onto the cold, wet sidewalk. Meanwhile, the littlest hoodlum retrieved Zinta's floppy dragon and waved it in the air like a trophy.

Mom's eyes met mine. I mouthed, "Fight." Then I dropped to the sidewalk, covering Zinta with my body.

A terrible, loud noise made my ears ring. The rest of the incident was a blur: *The cold cement. Shockwaves of heat. Voices screaming. High-pitched notes of breaking glass. The crackle of burning wood. The stench of burnt hair and flesh. Ronnie's protective arm across my back.*

The authorities believed a gas leak had caused the explosion that besieged our attackers. I knew better.

At the police station, I hugged my daughter to me as a young policeman offered my brother, my grandmother, and me a scripted consolation. "I'm sorry for your loss."

I caressed the outline of a hole burned into my mitten. Tears splashed the black-and-white stitches as I mourned our protector— my mother.

My *pukís.*

Oranka's Shells

Kristine Haecker

Your Honor, I have just been retained as Mr. Pern's lawyer. I would like to move for a dismissal of all charges."

I could hardly believe my ears. I had never seen this lawyer before, but apparently he had quite the pair. From the back row of seats in the gallery, I looked at Jenny, who sat at a table at the front. She'd been through so much, the hardest part of which was the type of abuse she had endured. Tom had never been physically abusive toward her. At least, never in a way that had required a trip to the hospital or had left any visible marks. I knew this would be a tough case for her, but moving for a dismissal was bold on the part of the defense.

"The state has no evidence of any wrongdoing. Furthermore, preventing my client from seeing his children is unnecessary and detrimental to their relationship."

I couldn't help the noise that came out of my throat then. Tom had no relationship to speak of with his kids. Whenever he wasn't working, he would berate Jenny for all the things she did wrong. He called it discipline, but that was a load of bull. It was about power and control, not care or concern.

"Counselor." The judge leaned forward, her eyebrows raised. "I think dismissing the case at this point in the process would be more detrimental to the defendant's wife and children than simply proceeding." The lawyer's mouth opened, but the judge raised her hand, stopping him. "Motion for dismissal denied." She banged her gavel. Looking between the two lawyers, she drew in a breath and sat back. "Anything further before we proceed?"

"Your Honor." I chuckled to myself at the sight of the judge's face as the voice of Tom's lawyer rang out again. "Since you have denied my motion to dismiss all charges, I request a continuance. As I said, I have only just been retained as Mr. Pern's lawyer, and I need some time to familiarize myself with the case."

"You need time to familiarize yourself with the case?" The judge leaned across the bench. "Not five minutes ago, you knew enough to move for dismissal."

"Your Honor, I apologize." He raised his hands in a sign of surrender. "I misspoke. I am familiar with only the basics of the case. I am requesting a continuance so I may prepare an effective defense."

His tone was oily, but there was something else about his voice. I squinted a little, staring at him intently as I tried to figure out what was niggling at my mind. He was a large man—solid, not fat—but he moved with surprising fluidity. His suit was a light navy instead of the typical black. Even from the back of the room, I could see his shoes were made from reptile skin, probably snake. Humans would call his hair raven black—so black, it was almost blue in certain light, a lot like my own hair. As I observed him, I only listened to the tone and tenor of his voice; the words didn't matter.

Realizing what I'd just thought, I shook myself and brought my attention back to the court proceedings. I needed to know exactly what was going on so I could best help Jenny through the process.

"I'll give you one week, Counselor. It would be less, but I only hear opening arguments for family court cases on Wednesdays." She paused and stared pointedly at Tom's lawyer. "Do not come ill-prepared next week." She nodded curtly. "No other motions?" She looked at each lawyer, then banged her gavel. "Court dismissed."

"Listen, it is going to be fine," I said, trying to reassure Jenny back at the shelter that afternoon. "One more week," I repeated for the third time.

"But, Liz, it's already been so long." I could hear the despair in her voice. "And the kids do ask where their dad is."

"No."

Jenny started, her eyes jumping to mine. "No, what?"

"No, you are not going back." Jenny's eyes widened. She was no doubt surprised I had picked up on what she hadn't yet said. "I have walked alongside more women than you can imagine—women in this exact position. It is always tempting to go back. Always. But don't romanticize your time with him."

I paused, trying to think how best to get through to her.

"Remember how many times he pulled your hair." I gave her a moment to think about it. "Or how many times he slapped you or spanked you, for that matter." Her eyes grew unfocused.

Damn human religions. Most taught women that they were "less than" from the time they could walk. It was probably the single hardest thing I had to fight against in my work. Untangling the threads that declared a "woman's place" was incredibly delicate work. However, I did know one thing that would put a steel rod down Jenny's back.

"Remind yourself how many times he threatened the kids." Her head snapped up as her back started to straighten. "How many times did he threaten to have you declared unfit and take them away?" Her shoulders pulled back. "How many times did he say you'd never see them again? That there was nothing you could do about it because you were nothing without him?" Her chin lifted, and I knew that steel rod of determination she needed was firmly back in place.

"He—was—wrong." I carefully enunciated each individual word. "You are many things without him. In fact, you are more without him than you ever were with him." She nodded. "And you have skills, talents, and abilities he will never be able to see. You can accomplish things without him. Look at the goals you have already set and achieved for yourself and the kids."

Tears welled in her eyes.

"Remember that. Keep it at the front of your mind." I smiled. "You still have the journal we had you start when you first got here?" She nodded. "Take some time before the kids get back from school and work through some more material."

She agreed, turning to head for her suite. I lifted an incantation to the Nesoi, the higher powers of my home world, to help her find her way.

Later that night, I made my rounds, helping my hoard of egglings— the children—settle into bed. As always, their haunted expressions reminded me of why I did this work.

I could still remember the first time I'd seen an eggling flinch away from an outstretched hand. I'd been coming out of a seedy office building after picking up a document I needed to build my life here on Earth. A woman and small child were going up the stairs as I came down. When the doorman lifted his hand to open the door for them, the little one flinched away. It had taken a moment for me to realize he was afraid the doorman would hit him. My hands flexed instinctively, reminding me—not for the first time—that I no longer had claws since coming to Earth.

For weeks, I couldn't get the expression of fear out of my mind. I started paying closer attention to the little ones I came across. I saw them most often on my visits to the library. Spending time in the children's section made me realize that humans couldn't feel the emotions and mental states of their little ones to the degree I could.

It wasn't until Tristan that I discovered I could do more for the egglings than just observe them.

I was stopping by my source's location to pick up some more documents, when I encountered Tristan and his mom on their way out of the office. His anguish took my breath away. It was so powerful, I nearly missed his mom speaking his name as she pulled him through the stairwell door. As they passed me on the stairs, I lifted a silent incantation to the Nesoi, asking them to protect the boy.

I didn't really expect much; like any higher power, the Nesoi were mysterious in their responses. So I was startled when something shimmered around Tristan. As soon as it closed around him in the shape of an egg, his body started to relax. And since his mother didn't react to it, I suspected humans wouldn't be able to see it.

That was the first shell I gave away.

It took a few more shells for me to realize how much I could truly help these little ones. Once I decided to pursue that course, I did everything I needed to be in a position to help as many as possible. I wove together all the documentation I needed so I could start a shelter, converting myself from Branka of Nereid to Liz of Earth.

A whimper pulled me from my memories. Looking in on one of the egglings, I could sense he was remembering something he should never have seen in the first place. I mentally checked the shell I had already placed around him for gaps or weaknesses. My shells didn't protect the egglings from physical harm or the outside world, but they did protect their minds. The shells prevented them from fully absorbing the bombardment of evil they faced at home.

Once everyone was settled for the night and the overnight crew had taken over, I went for a run. Most women thought I was insane for running in the middle of the night, but unlike them, I knew what I was capable of. Shells and empathy weren't the only traces of my old self that had translated to my new form when I came through the Janus Well. I might not have had wings or claws anymore, but I still had incredible stamina and nearly my full power and strength.

As my feet hit the pavement in an ancient rhythm, I replayed the hearing in my mind. The defense lawyer's arguments sounded through my head as though I were still in the courtroom. There had been something about his voice that had bothered me. His tone had been oily, but his voice had sounded rough, gravelly. Like the rumble of machinery. Something lower than the tones typical human voices reached.

I stopped dead in my tracks.

He sounded like home!

Was it possible? I had never heard another voice here on Earth that reminded me of home. Sure, I'd heard voices with similar qualities, but never that exact underlying pitch. It reminded me of my Dragent—my father—calling me home at the end of a day playing with my friends.

I forced myself to start walking again as I felt my muscles stiffen in the chilly night air.

I needed to get close enough to hear the lawyer's voice again as soon as possible, but I would need a legitimate excuse to do so. I pondered my options as I returned to the shelter, cleaned up a bit, and checked in on my hoard again before going to bed. Just thinking of the egglings as mine to protect brought a smile to my face.

I hadn't been able to come up with an excuse to see Tom's lawyer before the following Wednesday. Minutes before the hearing was set to start, I saw Jenny's husband and his lawyer coming down the hall. The lawyer had his head down and to one side, conferring with his client. I stood still in the hallway, waiting for him to look up. He never lifted his head, not even a centimeter, and he walked right into me. Stumbling back a half step, he jerked his head up, annoyance obvious on his face. Clearly, this was a man accustomed to being deferred to.

He might have met his match in me.

Then I saw his eyes. I had never seen eyes that shade of blue here on Earth. Or eyes that appeared to have a ring of actual fire around the pupil. As close as I was, I could have sworn the ring of fire was actually moving.

"I didn't see you there," he said. No apology, I noted.

"Clearly," I answered dryly.

"Excuse us," he said as they stepped past me. I barely suppressed a shiver when his voice reached into the deepest part of my brain—the reptilian part. My hands tensed, and my fingers spread wide. I was reminded, again, that I was no longer a dragon and didn't have claws.

The first hearing that Wednesday afternoon was simply routine, little more than opening arguments. The judge gave her usual spiel about what would and would not be tolerated in her courtroom. Then we were dismissed until the following morning, when evidence and lists of witnesses would be introduced.

That night, I sat in the common room of the shelter holding a now-cold cup of tea. Thoughts of who, or what, Tom's lawyer might have been were overwhelmed by my contemplation of the day's hearing.

Because there was no evidence of physical abuse, Tom's lawyer had claimed that the children were in no danger from their father. Therefore, supervised visitation was excessive and unnecessary. He didn't seem to care that everyone working with the children agreed that witnessing the abuse of their mother and living in that environment was traumatizing and a form of abuse itself.

Thank goodness we had Judge Maxins. Everyone in the state knew how tough she was on men who mistreated their wives and children. We needed a judge like her to ensure Jenny and her kids would be safe going forward. But still, as great as she was, Judge Maxins was still bound to the legal requirements of things like custody.

Throughout all the trial prep, there had only been one therapist who had managed to get Tom to talk at all in depth. That therapist had gone on record to say that Tom had significant narcissistic tendencies, that he didn't have a genuine desire for actual relationships with anyone, much less with a wife or children. I hoped that would be enough for Judge Maxins, but without physical evidence, it might be difficult to argue for supervised visitation.

For once, I really didn't know how things were going to turn out.

The next day, I stood in the hallway waiting for Jenny to exit the courtroom. As they came out, she and her attorney were discussing the case and how things had gone so far. The case did not seem to be falling clearly in favor of either side.

Tom and his lawyer came out just behind Jenny and her attorney. When he spotted me, Tom's lawyer made his excuses to his client and walked over to me. He stretched out a hand for me to shake. I hesitated but quickly decided to stick with the customs of this world in case he was just an unusual human.

The moment our hands touched, something like electricity jolted up my arm. Seemingly unfazed, he smiled.

"Hello, my name is Janus Bragent. I don't believe we've formally met."

Something in his smile and tone had me tugging my hand out of his. Bragents were the Nereid equivalent of brothers, and Janus had been the name of the dragon from the Nesoi legend about the well that brought me to Earth. The well my friends had dared me to touch, even though we had been warned throughout our lives of its dangers.

"No," I agreed. "We haven't."

"Your name?"

"Liz."

"I think we both want the same thing here." He smiled, his tone as oily as ever, and his expression condescending.

"No, I don't think we do." I crossed my arms. His smile widened.

"Well then, I hope we can find some common ground." He raised one eyebrow and lowered his voice. "Or I may just invoke the Nesoi to push this judgment in my favor."

My lips parted with a gasp. In all my years here on Earth, I had never heard anyone mention the Nesoi.

"Go ahead," he added. "Ask me."

"Ask you what?"

"Ask me where I'm from."

"Where?" I didn't want to play his game, but I would do what I had to, to have him gone. The ancient part of my brain screamed that it wanted him gone permanently.

"Nereid, where the Nesoi are the Keepers," he answered, voice still quiet.

My eyes widened. I could hardly believe what he was saying. If he was the Janus of legend . . . but he looked no older than me, so how could that be? How long had he been here?

"We should talk," he said, interrupting my racing thoughts. "Meet me at the café along the square downtown, Saturday morning at nine." I nodded, unable to speak. He nodded once, his smile appearing as oily as his tone had been, and walked away.

I spent the next days reeling, trying to determine what any of this could mean. By Saturday morning, I had reached no appealing conclusions.

I arrived at the café a few minutes early. Janus was already seated at a table on the sidewalk veranda outside. He rose as I approached and held the door as I entered. I gave the barista my simple order. Looking over the pastries, I decided I wouldn't be able to eat. As I did, Janus gave his surprisingly complex order.

Before I could think about it, Janus pulled out his wallet and paid for both drinks. I protested, but he waved me off. I subsided, deciding that between his initiation of the meeting and the ridiculous price of his nonsense drink, it only made sense for him to pay for mine.

When our drinks came up, we returned to the table outside.

"How are you?" he asked as soon as we were settled. "How are things back home?"

"I'm fine," I answered automatically. My brows pulled together as the second question registered. "I've no idea how things are back home; I haven't been there in ages."

"Ah, but you've been there since I left, yes?" He sipped at his drink.

"If you're the Janus of legend, that was centuries before I was even an eggling."

"So how long have you been here?"

I squinted as I tried to remember when I had first arrived and calculate the time between then and now.

"I think about thirty years." I shrugged. I hadn't kept careful track in the beginning.

"And you didn't arrive as an eggling or small child? You arrived full-grown, yes?"

"Yes." Another automatic answer. I didn't like that, but I didn't know why I was doing it. "How long have you been here?" I said, turning the question on him.

"One hundred years, I think. It's tough to keep track, though after I got my bearings, it wasn't so bad."

"Holy crap!" He didn't look a bit older than me. How could he have been here a hundred years? "I didn't even think you were real. I thought you were just a story dragents told their egglings to make them behave."

His brows drew together as his eyes met mine. "My theory has been that we age at the same rate as we would back home. Since Earth is closer to the sun than Nereid is, Earth years pass much faster. But if I was already legend in your time, maybe I've been here longer than I thought."

"What have you been doing?"

He responded with a creepy, oily smirk. "Making money, building my hoard, staking out my territory, and protecting it."

"From what?"

He shrugged. "From anyone who wants to take it from me."

I let my mind turn over the implications of Janus being here. "Then why haven't I seen you before?"

"I just moved to this area. I had accumulated all I could where I was." He glanced sideways. "Plus, the humans were getting suspicious of my lack of aging."

He paused. "I may have been here longer than I thought, actually. I wasn't paying much attention when I first arrived. I spent far too long looking for a well that would bring me back home. I've had to move a few times since I gave up looking. I guess it would all add up to more than just one hundred."

"What do you want?" I blurted out.

His gross oily smirk came back. "I thought we could join forces. It appears we're the only two of our kind here. We could build something spectacular."

My skin crawled. "If the legend about you is true, then you don't exactly play well with others. Nor do you abide by rules very well."

"That is true." He chuckled. "But that has served me well here."

"I couldn't possibly join with you."

"Why not?"

I considered how to explain it in a way he might comprehend.

"I see value in them as individuals," I finally answered. "I see the incredible potential of the egglings. And I have no desire to accumulate wealth for its own sake."

He nodded, his smile not even faltering. "I thought that might be the case. Whereas, I see them as nothing more than pawns, tools to accumulate my wealth, the means to my end."

He sighed. "We'll need to come to some kind of agreement." My brows drew together. Before I could ask my question, he added, "If you think they have individual value and I see them only as pawns, we're going to have some conflicts. If I stay in this area—and I intend to—then we'll be tripping over one another."

"You intend to stay? Even though this area is already claimed?"

I hadn't even realized the words were true until they were spilling from my lips. I had unconsciously laid claim to all the area I could see from where I now resided. There had been no one to challenge it before, no one to defend it from, but now, ancient rivalries stampeded to the forefront of my mind. Again, my hands flexed, readying claws that were not there. I wondered what strengths Janus still possessed from his trip through the well.

"I have been on Earth far longer than you," Janus replied, "and I know how much work it takes to resettle myself. Yes, I am staying. I have already relocated my hoard, and I like my new home and this area. I do quite a bit of research before I move. It would take too much time and effort to find fresh territory. Plus, we have very different goals and could coexist quite nicely."

It was logical, but something in it rang alarm bells in my ancient brain.

"Why don't we give it a try and see what happens?" he finished.

I looked at him, trying to see through the rotating fire in his eyes. I tried to see into his mind, to figure out what his intentions were. He simply looked back at me, waiting.

"That won't work."

"Why not?"

"Because you want to destroy everything I've built."

"Come now, that seems a bit dramatic."

"It's not. Your client is trying to harm innocents of my hoard. I can't allow that."

"Ah . . . so that's your hoard. The egglings!" He chuckled. "I'd been wondering about that since our talk at the courthouse. You didn't seem wealthy by this world's standards. Good to know you won't be fighting me for the wealth in this region." He chuckled again.

"No, but if you continue in the life you've chosen, then we'll not only trip over one another, we'll be in constant conflict."

He thought about this for a minute or two.

"That could be true. Perhaps we can reach an agreement of sorts? A truce?" I immediately shook my head. "I thought you'd say no but wanted to offer it anyway. It appears we're at an impasse, then." I eyed him warily. "I propose we go our separate ways and battle it out when we cross paths next. Perhaps one of us will come up with a compromise between now and then?"

I shrugged. "I don't see any possibility of compromise between us when we're so categorically opposed."

"Nor do I, but one never knows what the future holds."

He stood and walked away. I stayed seated long after he had left, my mind reeling and stunned at the same time. I needed to go for a run; I did my best thinking when I was running. I needed to figure out some kind of solution; I could not let him use my hoard as pawns for his greed.

"Your Honor, really!" Jenny's lawyer yelled.

Jenny was on the witness stand, and I was doing my best to send her calm and strength. However, her eyes darted around and the pulse pounded in her throat, and I could see it wasn't working. Janus was cross-examining her, asking her questions that were hardly more than riddles. She was getting twisted up trying to answer.

The gavel banged.

"The counselor is grand standing," her lawyer continued heedlessly. "Is there even a question in there?" He paused. "A legitimate question?" He looked at the defense attorney.

"So far, he has spoken a couple dozen sentences full of double negatives. Not to mention, he's implied that my client is unfit and that this hearing is a waste of everyone's time."

I took in the look on the judge's face. She didn't like what Janus was doing either, but he was still technically inside the bounds of the courtroom. Jenny's lawyer, on the other hand, was now sailing perilously close to the wind. Thankfully, he noticed the judge's expression as well and shut his mouth.

I looked at Jenny. Her eyes were still, but her pulse hadn't slowed. I willed her to look at me; when she did, I mouthed counting out of order. It was a technique I had seen on TV. If someone was experiencing a panic attack, counting out of order confused their brain and calmed them. I watched her shoulders move as her breathing slowed.

Out of the corner of my eye, I noticed Janus looking at me. I ignored him, instead watching as Jenny's pulse slowed. I could tell she was breathing more deeply, and I hoped she was repeating her mantras.

"Counselor, get on with it," the judge finally said, looking to Janus. "Make your point or sit down."

I sat in the back of the courtroom, trying to figure out how else I could help Jenny. I wished I could protect her from everything, but even just protecting her from Janus right now would have been fantastic.

I squinted a bit as something shifted and shimmered around her on the stand. I let my eyes shift and go out of focus to see if it was my eyes acting up. It wasn't my eyes; a transparent ovoid seemed to enclose her entirely.

Suddenly, I registered that Janus's tone changed. I shifted my attention to him.

Jenny was now refusing to play his game. When he asked a question, she paused, took a breath, considered the question, and replied as simply as she could. I could have done cartwheels!

Then it dawned on me: I had done that! My wish to protect her had created a shell around her, like the ones I had been putting around my egglings. I had never tried it on an adult.

When Janus had finished his questions, he sat down, allowing Jenny to return to her seat. The shell followed, fully intact.

"Oh, Liz, thank you so much," Jenny effused, interrupting my musings outside the courtroom after the hearing. "I could see you mouthing the numbers at me, and I swear I could feel your strength filling me up!"

I smiled and hugged her, then put my arm over her shoulders and led her out of the courthouse, into the sunshine.

"I gotta go," she said. "I can't wait to see the kids. I hate being away from them!"

"I know," I agreed. "Go on. I can see the hood of Mr. Randall's car just over there." I barely tilted my head toward the street corner. "I'll watch and make sure you get in okay. Tell him I've got errands to run, so you don't need to wait for me."

Mr. Randall was a large, extremely fit dark-skinned man whom I had hired as a bodyguard for the shelter. He was truly a gentle giant, unless you messed with someone he considered family. Since starting at Branka's House, he had given so many women and children a new hope that there were good men in the world who would never hurt them.

"Thank you again," she said, shaking my hand. She bounced down the stairs to the car. I watched them drive off, then tilted my face up to feel the sun on my skin.

"You win this round," came Janus's voice from behind me.

"Oh?" I asked. "I don't know what you mean." I cocked my head to the side, as if confused.

"Oh, you know exactly what I mean. I saw the shell you gave her." Something in my expression must have given me away because he added, "Don't worry. No one else could see it, not unless they were also from Nereid. But it does give me a few ideas."

My stomach dropped. What could he do with similar abilities? What kind of damage could he inflict?

"For now, though, I've decided to shift my practice away from family court. I may have been on Earth longer, but I concede that this is claimed territory. You clearly have sway and influence I can't compete with." He bowed to me mockingly and walked away.

I couldn't decide whether to believe him. Could I trust him? He had already said he wasn't going to move from this area.

I shrugged then, letting it go. I had won this round. I needed to eat and go for a run. Those were the two biggest things that I had found recharged me and allowed me to keep working at the shelter.

I would focus on today now and only deal with Janus, and the implications of his statements, when we next crossed paths. I would stay in top form, though, so I could be as strong as possible when that time came.

Mine

Theda Vallee

Izzy pulled her cloak down over her forehead as the sun reached its zenith. It felt like an eternity since she'd stepped out of the tree-lined path and onto the dry, cracked earth that stretched endlessly in every direction. If she was counting correctly, it had been six sunsets since she'd left behind the freehold that had been her home since birth.

Her village stood as the last bastion of civilization before the vast swath of nothing she now found herself traversing. Rumor had it that no one lived in this space anymore, except the Bollywoggers. They were a nomadic tribe of people who scavenged off the ruins of cities that had been decimated long before Izzy was born. As far as she was concerned, they could bloody well have it.

Sweat trickled down the indent of her spine as she forced herself to move forward, one foot at a time. She licked her lips, wincing in pain as her tongue skated across the deep fissures that had formed around her mouth. Thirst was a constant gnawing entity out here, making it difficult to conserve the skins of water she'd brought along. The longer she trudged through the madness-inducing heat, the more her mind wandered to the stream just outside the village's walls. She longed to dive into its crisp, cool waters and drink until her belly bulged.

She squinted, her chestnut-colored eyes straining to see the outline of the person she'd been following. The woman's lean form was a dot in the distance. She'd hoped the woman would seek shelter during the day, but instead, she trudged forward relentlessly, her stride punishing the hard-packed earth as she pushed on.

A week ago, Bollywoggers had invaded the woods behind Izzy's village. They took five children. The people of the freehold had grown lax in the years since the woman had come. Izzy was too young to remember, but she'd heard stories from the old-timers. Before the woman, no one had been safe. The children never would've been allowed in the woods alone. But they had forgotten. Forgotten what had brought the woman to their gates in the first place.

Izzy was free. It was more than could be said for most of the world. She'd been born into one of the last thirteen colonies that dared to stand against the Corporations, or Corps, as they swept across the continent. When laws were enacted that gave the Corps statehood, they grew ruthless in their quest to acquire and consume.

At first, they bought what they could. When they were met with resistance, they simply took what they wanted. Some of the displaced people were given jobs in the Corp cities. They were whisked away to live in the encapsulated paradises created for employees. The rest became "recruits"—a palatable term for the horror they'd eventually become.

The Corp armies raced around the globe razing villages, but a few defied them. Izzy's village had chosen to stand firm. They would have rather died than be altered beyond their humanity. Long ago, her great-grandparents had stood on the wall surrounding the village, aiming useless weapons at the invading forces. Freeholds weren't allowed to acquire guns. They only had what their ancestors had passed down or the few items that had been scrounged on the black markets. It wouldn't have been enough to stop the hundreds of soldiers that marched toward their home.

The woman had arrived that day. She had looked and acted like the other soldiers, her mind seemingly no longer her own. The Corps had found a way to erase every trace of humanness, leaving their recruits as mindless tools.

The woman had been different, though. Somehow, she overrode the programming and made a choice they didn't think she was capable of. She chose to save the people of the village.

The engineers had been complacent. They had never dreamed their creations would stop following orders. As far as they had been concerned, their code was infallible. When the woman had turned on the other recruits, the ranks collapsed into chaos. There was no protocol in their command logic that accounted for one of their own being a threat.

Like the other recruits, the woman had been modified. She had microscopic turbines implanted in her hands that sucked in air, converting it into fuel that she used to wield fire on command. The cells of her body had been imbued with nanotech that allowed them to continue multiplying in perpetuity, stopping the normal aging process. The nanotech also gave her speed and strength that outmatched even the best warrior huddled behind the village walls.

Izzy had heard the tale a thousand times. The old-timers seemed to revel in the gruesome imagery from that day. They said the woman had stood among the carnage, watching as a ring of fire greedily consumed the hundreds of bodies that had succumbed to her wrath. She had remained motionless for hours, waiting to ensure that every last soldier burned in her flames. When she was satisfied the job was done, she'd flung her head back, sending a shower of gore through the air, and let lose a savage roar.

"Minnnnnnnnne!"

Mine. The only word they'd ever heard her speak. Afterward, she'd slunk off to a forgotten clapboard cottage nestled outside the village. Some of the braver folks had tried to befriend her, their curiosity driving them to her door bearing gifts. Their efforts had never yielded more than growls and grunts, the woman's demeanor more animal than human. In the end, they kept their distance, grateful she'd decided the village was hers to protect. She had kept them safe all these years, until the Bollywoggers took the children from the forest last week.

When Izzy had heard her brother was among the missing, she'd grabbed an antiquated rifle, a few skins of water, and a handful of rations before heading after the woman. It wasn't in Izzy's nature to stay home praying to the Seven Mothers, hoping he'd be returned unharmed.

She was beginning to regret her rash decision as she stumbled up a rocky incline.

At the crest of the hill, Izzy froze. Crouched on the edge, overlooking the canyon below, was the woman. Her hands were pressed against the ground, flickering with flames, as a low, menacing growl rolled out from her diaphragm. Her body sizzled with unused energy.

"Hello," Izzy said, hoping not to startle the woman.

In reply, the woman flipped up from the ground in one fluid movement, her body snaking across the distance between them within seconds. "Go," she hissed, the word sounding alien as it crossed her lips.

Izzy stepped forward, her lanky frame trembling. She'd spent sixteen seasons on this earth and had never had reason to fear the woman. Yet terror clouded her mind as she eyed the woman warily. This half-wild woman was their champion, but feral beasts would attack those who thought to tame them.

"No. My brother was taken. There's nowhere else I should be." Izzy met the flat gray eyes of the woman.

"Mine." The woman smacked her chest. "Go."

"I can help. I can hit a target up to a mile away." Izzy patted the black rifle bag slung over her shoulder. "You'll need help with the children on the way home. I can do that."

The woman invaded the small pocket of space between them. She towered over Izzy, pressing her palms into Izzy's shoulders. The woman pushed, trying to force the girl back the way she'd come. Digging her heels into the ground, Izzy pushed back, allowing stubbornness to infuse her body with renewed strength. She would bring her brother home, with or without the woman's help.

Feeling the resistance, the woman stopped. She cocked her head to the left, studying Izzy's face. Tilting her head from side to side, she let a grin spread across her lips. Slowly, her hand reached out, tenderly cupping the side of Izzy's face. "Mine," she said, the word coming out a whispered benediction.

Izzy nodded, trembling under the unexpected touch. The woman's smile widened, contorting and overextending her features. She dropped her hand and motioned for Izzy to follow. Plopping onto her stomach, the woman crawled to the edge of the canyon.

The canyon spread out for miles in either direction, wide enough for a dozen or so cars to fit side by side. The Bollywoggers had set up camp on the far side. The children had been unloaded and corralled into one corner of their makeshift camp. Three armed guards kept watch over them. The rest of the crew had set up a perimeter near their vehicles. Six campfires glowed softly every hundred feet or so.

Izzy quickly estimated the number of people they were facing. Each car would have held five or six men. Whatever the legends surrounding the woman, Izzy felt the immense weight of their task. Two women. One rifle. Thirty-five heavily armed men. It seemed impossible.

Inhaling deeply, Izzy wiggled back and forth in the dirt, trying to force the ground to contour around her. "What do you need me to do?"

The woman patted the rifle bag on Izzy's back and pointed to the line of vehicles. "You want me to lay down cover fire?" she whispered. The woman bobbed her head in agreement.

"Okay. Create a diversion so you can sneak in and get the kids. Got it." Izzy removed her rifle from its case, working with practiced hands to position it. "What are you going to do?"

The woman pulled herself up into a crouch. Her face oozing menace, she waved at Izzy and dropped off the edge of the cliff. Izzy gasped, certain the woman had just leaped to her death. She scrambled to the ledge, peering over with trepidation, expecting to see the woman in a crumpled heap. Instead, she watched in awe as the woman drifted to the ground in a graceful arc, landing with ease at the bottom.

The woman took off running across the packed dirt, her legs churning with inhuman speed, covering the distance to the camp in the time it took Izzy to lick her parched lips.

Forcing herself to focus on her task, Izzy looked down the scope, searching for the lead vehicle. Spotting the heavily armored pickup truck, she aimed at the rear tire. She whispered a silent prayer to the Seven Mothers and slowly pulled the trigger.

Her shot went wide, spraying dirt through the air. The men huddling around their campfires leaped up, scrambling for their weapons. She fired off another shot, not bothering to aim this time. The point was to have them panicked, which worked like a charm. Chaos erupted as she fired her third shot. Rapid bursts of gunfire answered in return, as the men scattered for cover. They had no idea that what they should truly fear was creeping toward them through the brush.

A wall of fire illuminated the twilight sky, racing down the line of vehicles and creating a barrier between the men and the small area where the children were being kept. Izzy searched through the scope for the tall, lithe frame of the woman. She found her slithering across the ground toward the first cluster of frantic men. Quickly, Izzy squeezed off another round, aiming away from the woman's position.

Tilting the scope back to where she'd last seen the woman, a small strangled sound slipped from her lips. Bile rose in her throat as her eyes settled on the carnage left in the woman's wake.

Izzy had seen death before. Life in the freeholds was harsh, sending many to the arms of the Seven Mothers earlier than expected. But looking at the glassy eyes of someone who'd succumbed to illness didn't compare to witnessing what the woman had done. Perhaps the view wouldn't have undone her if it weren't for the accompanying sounds. She'd never known humans were capable of emitting the noises that drifted up to her as she lay trembling on the ridge.

The camp burned white hot against the sky. The heat from it settled over Izzy like a thick winter blanket. She peered through the scope, searching for signs of the children, as the thick smoke wafted up to her and stung her eyes. Finally, she spotted the woman stepping out of a thick black cloud, followed closely by five small shadows. The woman strode toward the cliff, her stride mindful of the little legs trailing behind her.

With fumbling hands, Izzy placed the rifle back in its bag. When the woman arrived, she needed to appear calm. The children couldn't see the terror that slithered along the underside of her skin. The woman had protected them since before she was born. There was no reason to believe that she would harm them now, despite the gruesome scene that lay stretched out below.

"Izzy!" her brother cried out as soon as the woman lifted him onto the ridge. She ran to him, wrapping her arms around his tiny body. Holding him against her, she allowed herself to cry for a moment.

The rest of the children ran to her one by one as they reached the top. Izzy was familiar to them from the village, a safe harbor in the storm they'd just weathered. She did her best to hold all of them, letting their tears soak through her shirt.

The woman stood off to the side, impatiently tapping her foot against the ground, letting Izzy know that the reunion wouldn't be allowed to continue much longer.

"We should camp here tonight. The children need rest," Izzy said to the woman once the crying had faded to intermittent sniffling.

"Go," the woman grunted, her hand gesturing toward the flames behind them. "More."

Izzy closed her eyes in frustration. The adrenaline that had kept her going was slowly leaving her system, allowing fatigue to overcome her. The woman was right, though. Bollywoggers left their women behind when they went scavenging. Someone would notice when these ones didn't check in, and that meant they'd come looking for their missing kin. When they found the devastation left below, they'd hunt whoever was responsible. Seven people trekking through the desert on foot would leave a trace, no matter how hard they worked to cover their tracks. There was no choice but to start walking.

Izzy nodded, releasing the children from her grasp. Crouching down to their level, she surveyed the bedraggled group. Three girls and two boys, all of them filthy from head to toe, but all of them alive. "I'm Izzy, Ezra's big sister. I know Marin and Astrid, but what are your names?"

The smallest girl of the bunch, with eyes the color of cinnamon, stepped forward. "I'm Marisol, and he's my friend Etienne," she said, pointing to the trembling boy beside her.

"Thank you, Marisol. I need you all to listen carefully. We have a long way to go before we get home. I need you to be brave. We don't have much water, and we'll have to find food as we go. It's going to be very hard. The most important thing is that you listen when me or the woman tell you something. We will get you home safely, but you have to listen and do whatever we say."

Marisol crept up to Ezra. Leaning close to his ear, she loudly whispered, "But what is her name?"

"She scares me," Marin whimpered.

"No, she's not scary. She saved you. She's the woman that protects our village." Izzy stood up. She walked over to the woman, stopping next to her. "Anyone outside our village should be afraid of her, but we never have to be."

It was a hard sell, looking at the woman as she stood on the ridge with the flames as her backdrop. She was covered in a grisly war paint of soot and blood. Her white hair was stained red, hanging in wet clumps as gore dripped into the dirt below. She looked like the stuff of nightmares.

Despite the macabre picture the woman presented, Marisol shuffled over to her. Marisol stuck her tiny hand out, tilted her chin up, and bravely made eye contact. "I'm Marisol. What's your name?"

The woman stared at the tiny outstretched hand, a look close to panic spreading across her face. She gingerly grasped the girl's hand, giving it an awkward pump, before snatching her hand back to her chest as if she'd been scalded. Her head shook back and forth as Marisol stood, waiting for an answer.

"I don't think she knows her name," Izzy said, as she took in the woman's look of confusion.

The children gasped in collective horror. Ten eyes settled on the nameless woman with pity. "We had a dog one time that we called Dog. Should we just call her Woman?" Astrid asked.

"Everyone deserves a name." Marisol fisted her hands on her hips. "If she doesn't remember, we'll give her one. Can we call you Sera? It was my grandmother's name."

The woman grunted, earning a smile from Marisol, who took that as acceptance.

With that settled, Izzy paired the children together, hoping they'd be easier to manage in twos. Taking Ezra's hand, she said a silent prayer to the Seven. She had a feeling they were going to need it.

Three days into their march toward home, and the children were holding up better than Izzy had expected. They slogged along with a joy only children seemed capable of. While Izzy constantly fretted about finding food and water for them, the children seemed focused on making the newly minted Sera smile or finding flowers in the barren earth.

There'd been no sight of anyone following them, which made Izzy nervous. Everything had been easy so far. If life had taught her anything, it was that the other shoe would always drop.

Always.

"I think we should stop here to rest," Izzy said when they had reached a lone crop of bushes that grew in the otherwise desolate landscape. They could use the brush for a fire to cook the lizards she'd caught. They'd tried having Sera cook some, but she tended to turn everything she touched to ash. Izzy had fed the children raw snake yesterday, hoping to stretch their meager water supply by absorbing what they could from the meat. That had resulted in more crying and gagging than she'd thought possible.

The woman ignored her, turning to the children to see who wanted to ride on her back for a while.

"Hey! I'm talking to you. We need to rest." Izzy planted her feet into the packed earth. The children froze, their large eyes staring at Izzy in horror, as if she'd let loose a string of curse words.

The woman made a chuffing sound, pointing in the direction of home. "No. Go."

"I'm tired. I've carried the children as often as you, and I'm not enhanced. My legs are human cells, no nanotech to speak of." She lifted her legs up and down to demonstrate their mortal frailty. "Let me rest for a few hours, and then we can push on. Please."

The woman's face softened as she bent her neck, looking down the length of her own body. She touched each of her limbs as if realizing her otherness for the first time. She held her hands up to her face, letting the fire dance across her fingers. A small melancholy sound crossed her lips as the fire died out.

"It's okay, Sera. We like your fire." Marisol wrapped her thin arms around the woman's leg. Craning her neck to look up, she gifted the woman with a broad toothy grin.

The woman dropped her hand to rest on Marisol's head, smoothing the hair away from her face. "Mine," she crooned.

"Come on, you can help me find rocks," Marisol said as she disentangled from the woman's legs. She grabbed Sera's hand, leading her toward a patch of dirt that looked promising. As they passed Izzy, the woman reached out, giving her arm a slight squeeze as if to reassure Izzy that she understood now.

Four more sunsets passed as they marched through the fractured wasteland, following the path toward home. They were covered in a fine layer of dust that coated their skin like a well-worn shirt. Their bodies cried out in pain as the desert evaporated the moisture from their very cells. They could feel the grit of sand on their teeth and the layer that coated their throats, leaving their voices raspy and weak when they tried to speak. The children spoke less and less as the days passed, their joy disappearing in the desert sun.

The first smattering of trees came into sight as they crested a small hill, sending a rush of adrenaline through them. The children cheered, throwing their hands into the air and waving their fingers in gleeful salute. Izzy knew that soon the sparse tree line would turn into a lush canopy, providing relief from the sun. A breeze would rustle through the leaves, cooling their sweat-drenched bodies. The very thought left Izzy feeling jubilant. She felt the tension that had ridden her like a wraith melt away. One more day and they'd be home.

Izzy turned to the woman, tugging her bottom lip between her teeth in an attempt to keep tears of relief from running down her face. "Thank you," she whispered.

"Mine." The word was followed by a small, almost human-sounding laugh.

"Ours," Izzy corrected, before running down the hill with outstretched arms, giddy with the promise of home.

They followed the worn trail leading to their village with a renewed sense of purpose. Izzy no longer felt the weight of her limbs fighting her with each step. It was as if the forest atmosphere buoyed both their spirits and their bodies. She'd thought the children were talkative before, but with the prospect of soft beds, warm baths, and full bellies so close, their exuberance echoed off the tree trunks, creating a melodic cacophony.

Izzy giggled as she watched Sera with her constant shadow, Marisol. The woman doggedly tried to master the skipping lessons the little girl had insisted on. If anyone from the village were to stumble on them, they'd never believe that the woman who had destroyed an entire army with fire and her bare hands could be the same creature clumsily trying to maneuver her legs at the behest of an adorable tyrant.

Izzy wondered if the woman would skulk back to her ramshackle cottage when they arrived home, or if perhaps she'd be able to convince her to stay in the village. In the last week, they'd become companions of a sort. The woman had learned a few words and seemed to enjoy being around the children. The townsfolk might balk at the idea of the woman living among them, but they were adaptable. Once they saw that she was still human under the animalistic exterior, they'd welcome her. If not, Izzy could be very persuasive.

The acrid tang of smoke filled Izzy's nostrils, snapping her out of her musings. The woman stopped midskip, slowly planting her dangling foot onto the ground. With a gentleness she'd not shown before, she pushed Marisol behind her. Raising her hand, she crooked her finger, beckoning Izzy to her side.

Izzy moved quickly, fear thrumming through her. She'd known the other shoe was going to drop, but she'd expected it to happen in the cursed desert, not this close to home.

The children stood silent, having learned to follow Sera's nonverbal cues. Her body was stiff and inflexible, a flurry of unspent energy bubbling around her aura. It was all the warning they needed. The woman hissed, softly nodding her head in the direction of home. Izzy understood precisely what she meant.

"Go. We'll follow behind. I'll hide the children in your cabin and then meet you."

The woman nodded, grabbing Izzy's hand and clutching it to her chest. She lifted the captured hand, nuzzling it to her cheek, and whispered, "Mine."

Izzy kept still, letting the woman infuse her with courage. Brusquely, she dropped Izzy's hand and launched into a dead sprint toward their home, leaving a spray of leaves in her wake.

Darkness had settled over the trees by the time they reached the cabin, but the orange flames burning in the distance made it feel as if they were still hounded by the wicked desert sun. Izzy herded the children inside the dilapidated building, kicking the bones that littered the floor into a corner, hoping the children wouldn't notice their grisly surroundings.

"Don't go outside unless me or Sera come back for you. If we don't come by morning, take my pack and follow the path going east. Keep walking until you find the next freehold; they'll help you."

Izzy knew the children would never survive the journey on their own. It took three weeks by horseback, and they had no supplies left. If she and Sera didn't return, it meant there was nothing left for them here. The children would either die on the road or die here. Better to send them down the road and hope they found a kindly stranger that would see them to safety.

Leaving the children behind, she made her way to the village. Thick waves of smoke enveloped her as she inched toward what remained of her home. The air burned her lungs as she tried to breathe normally, ignoring the weight of terror that crushed in on her from every direction.

She found the woman crumpled in front of the gates. Sera lay on the ground with her knees pulled to her chest. The sound of her keening intertwined with the soft pop and crackle of the fire, created a haunting melody that Izzy would never forget. Walking past her, Izzy stood at what had once been the main gate. She gazed down the street, cataloging the complete desolation of her home. There was nothing and no one left.

Izzy spotted a glint of silver buried in the trampled grass near the gate. She bent to retrieve it, hoping to preserve some last vestige of home.

She gasped as she peered at the muddied emblem. It was stamped with a Corp insignia. Stealing the children must have been a ruse. One of the Corps had finally figured out how to elude the woman. They had known she would chase after what she considered hers.

If that were true, then this had only been the first wave. They'd be back soon with their machines, ready to harvest everything that had once sustained her people. Within a year, her home would look like the desert they'd just crossed.

Izzy knelt beside the woman, brushing the hair back from her face. She ignored the hisses and snarls, knowing Sera wouldn't harm her. "We need to go. We have to take the children somewhere safe."

"Mine!" the woman screamed, pushing Izzy away. She leaped to her feet, beating her chest, screaming into the night air, as if that would return the people of the village.

"It was ours. Yours and mine, and it's gone. There is only me and the children left. We're still yours, and we need you. I need you, Sera. Help me take the children to the next village. We can't stay here. The Corp will be back, and this time, we can't fight them. This time, we have to run. Help me. Please."

Izzy stood in front of the woman, her legs threatening to give out. "I know it hurts. We loved them. They're part of us. The only thing we can do now is live so that we can remember them. Please. Help me live so I can remember them."

Izzy stood there raw with grief, reaching out to the only person who stood between her and death. Her tears burned hot trails down her face as she waited for the woman to respond.

Sera grabbed Izzy, pulling her tight against her body. She wrapped her arms around her in a crushing embrace. "Yes. Mine. Izzy." She repeated the three words over and over, letting tears of defeat fall on Izzy's shoulders until they ran dry.

With a final wipe of her face, she released Izzy. The two women linked hands and walked up the path toward the cabin. They took their time, moving with the leaden grace of a usurped monarch heading for the guillotine. Both women worked to tuck their pain away so they could face the children and give them the hope they'd need to endure.

When they reached the stoop, the children poured out of the cabin and down the steps, their dirty faces etched with fear.

"Can we go home now?" Ezra asked.

"Our home is gone. We have to leave, but Sera is going to help us find a new home." Izzy plastered a tight smile on her face.

"Are you our mother now?" Marisol asked, her bottom lip quivering as she looked at Sera.

Sera nodded, opening her arms for the children. They crowded around her, sniffling and sobbing as they mourned their home. "Mine," Sera said, tucking the collection of children against her.

Whatever she had been in her life before she came to them, she was now Sera, mother of the last surviving children of the Thirteenth Colony. And she would see her family to safety.

The Art of Courage

Deana Rose Wilson

Moon Song huddled deeper into the bushes and closed her eyes, concentrating on her breathing, her hands squeezing the smooth metal of her bow. Evergreen and sage filled her nostrils, and the sun freckled her through the trees. A meadowlark sang high in the branches. All signs of a picnic-perfect afternoon. She resisted the urge to snort. If only she weren't deep in enemy territory.

Focus.

Words drifted up from where they had been planted deep within her subconscious, and she exhaled them in a whisper like a mantra. "'The causes of defeat come from within; victory is born in the enemy's camp.'"

She opened her green eyes slowly, her pupils dilating as she scoured the stark fortress before her. It wasn't difficult, even with the sun setting. White watchtowers rose blatantly against the dimming evening sky, arrogant and seemingly impenetrable. Her fingers drummed silently across her bow as she counted the patrols on the battlements.

She scoffed. *If you want to call the wide walls around the fortress such an ancient term.*

Her eyes narrowed, and she tallied the nearly invisible security cameras that spanned the fortress, evenly spaced at each corner. A stirring of dust in a sudden breeze and the reflection of a floodlight drew her gaze to the line of an infrared sensor. She snorted again.

«Don't get cocky, Captain.»

The voice in her head would have startled her, but she was so attuned to Sun that she had known the chastisement was coming before he even pushed the words into her mind. She smirked and sent her own thoughts back through the mental link that bound them together as she raised a finger to test the direction and strength of the wind.

«'The flow of water is regulated by the shape of the ground; victory is gained by acting in accordance with the state of the enemy.'»

«'Shall I teach thee what is wisdom? To know what we know, and know *what we do not know*, is wisdom.'»

Moon rolled her eyes. «Are you calling me ignorant, my love?»

«I can't believe how ignorant *I* was to not understand your plan.»

Guilt tightened her chest. She could almost feel his pain through the link and bit her lip against it. She could hear the unspoken—or rather unthought—words. *Come back. Don't do this.* But the military training had been as deeply ingrained in Sun as it had been in her. He understood her motives and goals; he knew what was on the line. This might be the last chance for humankind to gain their world back.

The InRah had come in the middle of winter, when the snow was deep on the Rockies and the sun huddled behind dismal gray clouds. Moon hadn't been born when the aliens invaded Earth, but her mother said the war had been swift and brutal. The spindly Grays had unleashed a biological weapon that swept over the earth, killing over two-thirds of its inhabitants. Those who had remained, like Moon's mother, went into hiding. With global governments failing and the invaders enslaving any they tracked down, to survive was counted a victory.

But something unexpected and fortuitous had come from the bio-bomb. The offspring of the survivors, like Moon, were born with varied and unique gifts. Some were pyrokinetic or hydrokinetic.

Moon had met a teen with telekinesis. Many, like her and Sun, could speak to each other over long distances using their minds. She had never met an actual telepath who could read minds, but General Williams had. Gifts of superior intelligence were rare but treasured and put to the greatest use for the Rebellion. Zoomer's ability to control technology had created a sensation in the compound when he arrived with his sister, an electrokinetic.

When their parents had learned about the gifts of the New Gen, they slowly began to band together with hope. The Underground Army Training Facility was set up near what was once Great Falls, Montana, hidden in the empty missile silos and their command centers. The underground structures had been abandoned since the Disarmament Act of 2037. With the aid of newcomers and their gifts, the silos were joined together with long submerged tunnels. Dorms were added as the number of recruits grew. Colonel Kim insisted on the building of an engineering lab, to which he conscripted Zoomer immediately. Moon's own mother insisted on the library.

She snapped out of her reverie. *All the more reason to stay the course, to protect what we have left.* She swallowed her guilt, feigning lighthearted sarcasm instead. «'These are the secrets of the successful strategist—'»

«Do *not* quote Suntzu to me as an explanation.»

She could feel his frustration and changed tactics. This time, the sarcasm was real.

«If the flappers weren't hell-bent on destroying our history and culture, I wouldn't have his words swimming in my head. And you wouldn't have Confucius in yours. You can blame them.»

As part of their campaign for power, the leaders of the aliens, the Big Heads with their swollen craniums, had methodically destroyed any trace of human society, starting with the state capitals and moving little by little on to libraries and schools in every town. As a child, Moon had seen the burning of the books at the library in Billings, watching helplessly from the vantage of a nearby decimated bank tower.

When Zoomer created the bibliochip in an effort to rescue

humankind's written word before the InRah could destroy it, Moon had been the first to volunteer. At least forty volumes were buried in her subconscious, turning her into a human archive. If she were to die, the chip would automatically download her library into other carriers.

Some of the New Gen were content to just safeguard the culture locked in their skulls. Others, like Sun and Moon, dipped into the words and learned from them. Although Moon had over forty volumes in her head, she drew on Suntzu's words like hymns. She believed they were the reason she had moved so quickly up the ranks. She had never once allowed herself to think it might be because Major Dance was her lover.

«Report, Captain?»

Good. Back to business. She could feel the exasperation in his thoughts, but at least he'd given up on trying to talk her out of her mission. *For now.*

She loved being with Sun. He was what her mom called surfer-boy gorgeous and brilliant to boot. But sometimes he was more serious about their relationship than she was ready for. Let the engineers and scientists take on the repopulation duties. She had a war to fight.

«I see four patrols of two Grays each. Another fifty drilling in the courtyard. There are a couple of Big Heads watching over them, but unless they're out on missions, it looks like the majority have gone home. Or wherever they came from.»

«It's pretty rare to see a Big Head leading a raid. That's what they have the Grays for. There may be more within the compound, though.»

«Well, that's the goal, isn't it? To find out?»

«I thought the goal was to destroy them before they could send out a distress signal for reinforcements. According to Abdul, the slave colony in Boston is manned by a skeleton crew of Grays. He said it's the same across the nation. The war is over; the generals have moved on, leaving outposts behind to finish the job and control the slaves.»

Moon rolled her eyes. «I was at the briefing, Major.»

«Then you know how dangerous this mission is.»

The unspoken words were there again. *You shouldn't have volunteered. You're too important. Come back. I love you.*

She took a deep breath and steeled herself, sitting up in the bushes and taking a knee. «I'm the only one who could make this shot at this distance, babe, and you know it.»

Thankfully, he didn't answer, and she closed her eyes, sucking in another calming breath. Closing the link as much as she could, she exhaled. Her eyes snapped open and focused on her target. Her projectiles were silent and invisible, sound waves guided by her bow at such a high frequency that only a dolphin could have heard it.

The first sonic arrow hit the left watchtower's camera. The second took out the infrared. The third rocked the fortress wall at the base, creating a giant crack in the white stone. She managed a fourth, nearly rupturing the wall, before the Grays were upon her, beating her into blackness with their electrosticks.

Water hit her face and torso like an ocean wave, icy and hard enough to rock her off-balance. She knew two things before she even opened her eyes: She was suspended from an overhead hook, shackled at the wrists. And she was completely naked.

A gurgling growl sounded to her near right, and she was slapped in the face, hard. "Wake up, hu-mon," a voice snarled.

Moon thought about keeping her eyes shut, but a slap to the other side of her face convinced her that the interrogation would come no matter what. She dug deep, recalling her mission and clinging to her training, and opened her eyes.

The creature before her was uglier than she had ever imagined he would be. Her mother had described them as humanoid, with enormous heads and eyes as black as ink. She had never mentioned that their heads were soft and swollen, like rotten melons. Or that the lilac-gray membrane that covered their skulls pulsated as they breathed.

A long scar curled the upper lip of the alien, giving it a permanent sneer. Fetid breath seeped from the opening. She waited for it to blink, for its all-black eyes to give her a moment of release. But the creature had no lids, and the shiny black eyes burrowed into her as though the beast were trying to burrow into her soul.

Maybe it is. Maybe it could read her mind. The thought chilled her, and she all but severed her link to Sun, keeping only a thread between them, a golden path back to all that was good.

Moon slid her gaze past the Big Head, studying the layout behind him. The room she was in was sterile, as white and cold as an operating room in a hospital. The image was completed by a table laid out with an array of sinister surgical instruments. She couldn't help the shiver that trembled through her whole body.

A second Big Head stood a few feet behind the first, turning her bow in his skinny, abnormally long-fingered hands. Beyond him was an open door, and it was there her attention was drawn. She could make out blinking control panels and the electronic display of a map. From the landmarks on it, she recognized the Great Salt Lake. A sweep of red covered the bottom portion of the map, and she could only assume that was the area the aliens had already explored, searching and conquering as they went. A brief warmth filled her chest as she saw how much of the north still remained unscathed.

"What are you doing here, hu-mon?" Big Head Number One asked, bringing her attention back to the dreaded inquisition. His voice was deep, like a wild animal's snarl, and his accent clipped the English, except for the pronunciation of her race. He dragged the word out with as much contempt and disgust as Colonel Kim addressing a newly conscripted grunt.

Guilt instantly pricked her. The colonel should never be compared to these murdering monsters. Monsters who she vowed would never see her fear. She managed her best smirk, despite what she could only imagine was a bruised and swelling cheek.

"Just came to see how many of you ugly flappers I could kill," she said. She let the taunt—a reference to the aliens' flipper-like hands—spit from her mouth like a curse.

If her enemy had been human, he might have frowned in return. She was unprepared for the alien's cold, clinical reaction as he jabbed the electrostick into her ribs and shocked her again. She screamed as the current swept like a spasm through her body. She could smell her skin burning, could hear it sizzle. The second Big Head, noting her attention to the control room, slowly and deliberately closed the door. Then he joined the first Big Head, still turning and studying the bow in his hands.

BH1 stepped aside, curling his long hands around the electrostick, his head bowing slightly to the other. Moon didn't miss the movement; her torturer was a subordinate to this Big Head. She now faced the head Big Head. Despite the pain still coursing through her ribs, she chuckled at her own inner joke.

"Yet your targets were very carefully chosen." HBH stepped closer still, his obsidian eyes boring into her, his breath hot on her face. His English was much better than her torturer's, almost too perfect, as if he had studied the language. "You were not shooting at us. You hit your targets. And this technology is too new for the hu-mons we conquered nineteen years ago." He leaned so close, she could make out a myriad of pale purple veins through the thin membrane that covered his pulsing skull. "How many are with you?"

"It's just me, you stupid f—"

The jolt hit her in the buttock, and she nearly bit through her tongue. Tears sprang into her eyes as blood filled her mouth. Moon was starting to think the aliens were incapable of smiling, but she swore HBH's eyes took on a satisfied glint.

"This doesn't have to be painful, hu-mon," he purred. "Tell me what I want to know, and you can go to the mining colony. Now, how many in your group?"

Moon closed her eyes and dug up every line of Suntzu's writing from her subconscious, running the mantra through her head like a song. She spat blood onto the ground and glared up at the alien.

"'In ancient times the rise to power of the province of Yin was due to Ichih, who was sent to the country of Hsia. Likewise during the foundation of the state of Chu—'"

She swore she saw the skin above HBH's eyes furrow before the electricity coursed through her again. Gasping, she forced her eyes open, forced herself to take in all the information she could. She swallowed hard when BH1 reached for a serrated blade but pushed the words through her chattering teeth.

"'Likewise during the foundation of the state of Chu, Luya lived among the people of Shang.'"

Sun pressed his index fingers into his throbbing temples and massaged them, his eyes squeezed tightly shut against the glare of the fluorescent lighting that illuminated the underground compound. He nearly jumped out of his skin when Colonel Kim tapped the desk in front of him with his pen.

"Anything, Major?" the elderly man asked.

Colonel Kim had been a retired Army veteran when the InRah invaded. Now, nineteen years later, the New Gen leaned on him as a leader, even though he could barely lift a rifle. With his guidance, they had established a strict training regimen, a hierarchy of officers, and a code of honor.

And a system of code names. No one knew the colonel's real name—not even the leaders of the Rebellion. Colonel Kim believed there was power in a name; it was best not to allow the enemy to subvert that power. Only Sun's parents still called him Alex. A testament to his skills despite his age, Kim Park knew every New Gen by name and ability. And he had few qualms about positioning them to the greatest advantage.

Years ago, fanatics would have called the colonel's tactics "exploitation." Those who had survived the InRah invasion called it "necessity."

Sun sighed. "I get bits and pieces. She's obviously in a great deal of pain. But she's managed to shut the link down to a pinhole." He rubbed a hand over his eyes again. It had been forty-eight hours. He hadn't slept since Moon had been captured. "I think she's actually trying to protect me."

"What kind of information?"

Sun inhaled and sat up straighter. So this was going to be an official report.

"I catch snatches of Suntzu's words. She must be using them to focus her mind—'Allure the enemy by giving him a small advantage. Confuse and capture him. . . . Make him angry, and confuse his plans. Pretend to be inferior, and cause him to despise you.'" Sun sighed again. "I know she has given him the false reports about our numbers, both the ones she created"—he met Colonel Kim's eyes, his heart like lead in his chest—"and the false information we fed her."

The colonel's feet shifted slightly, but otherwise he remained cool and reserved. Sun huffed with disgust and looked away. But the words of Confucius rose in his mind. *If a man were to give his strength to love for one day, I have seen no one whose strength would fail him.'* And Moon was always in his heart. He straightened his shoulders and faced his superior officer again.

"Are Major Fleche's troops in place?"

Colonel Kim arched an eyebrow but allowed the insubordination. "They have been since last night."

Sun exhaled in relief. "I keep hearing one phrase over and over, Colonel. I'd like to make it a reality."

"What's that, Major?"

"She keeps repeating, 'Living spies return to report.'"

Moon forced her eyes open. There wasn't one inch of her body that didn't hurt. She'd been beaten, burned, flayed, sliced, and diced. She managed a lopsided grin despite the split in her lip. *Like a chicken filet when Sun lets me cook. That's how I feel. Maybe he better do the cooking from now on.*

HBH and BH1 were gone, and she exhaled with relief. Her right eye was swollen shut, but through the blur of her left eye, she caught the light and flicker of movement from the control room. A Gray had checked in on her and left the door open! She blinked several times, and the film finally cleared from her eye. Frantic, she forced open her mental link to Sun, flooding information through it like a spillway opening in a dam.

Sun stood upright so quickly, he smacked his head on the piping in the ceiling.

"Sh-she—she's sending information," he stammered, his words loud, though they were drowned out by the mental hum in his head. Out of the corner of his eye, he saw Colonel Kim scramble for a pen in his pocket. "She can see the panel that shows where the enemy is deployed across North America. And the locations of *all* the mining colonies. I have them saved to my bio-nodule. Only two troops are stationed at the fortress, fifty Grays per troop. And only the two Big Heads. She can see the communication array."

He blinked, focusing his eyes. "Colonel, she's going to take it out. Send word to Fleche. Tell him to attack now!"

Moon's arms and shoulders ached from the weight of her body hanging from them. But the careless Gray had created the opportunity she had been waiting for. An open door to the control room and a perfect view of their map. She was sure they thought she was nearly dead. Thank God for Colonel Kim's survival and espionage training. And thank God the HBH didn't know she could read InRah. Now to see if Major Steel's gymnastic training would prove useful.

Several blows to the face and one strangulation had given her opportunity to see her restraints, but she rolled her head back to re-evaluate them, ignoring the sudden throbbing that made her vision flash. A simple S-hook, used for hanging meat, secured her manacles to an overhead water pipe. She closed her mind to her ripping tendons and bruised muscles and pulled her legs up, twisting her torso until her feet were above her hands. She managed to shimmy herself up far enough that she could catch a knee over the pipe.

Supporting herself with that knee, she slid the manacles off their hook and grabbed it with her hands. Dropping her weight back onto her fatigued shoulders almost made her scream aloud. Nearly biting through her lip, she managed to drop soundlessly to the ground.

«I'm going, Sun.» She sucked in a deep breath and bunched her legs beneath her like a racer. «Attack now.»

She didn't wait for an answer but exploded into the control room. The two Grays she found there reacted too slowly, rising from their seats in surprise. By the time they made their feet, Moon had already slammed her manacles against the control panel at the communication station. Sparks flew around her, and a glass-like material splintered beneath the metal of her manacles.

She didn't think twice. She curled her hands around a sharp piece of the substance and slashed at the nearest Gray's throat. He fell to the floor, his long hands trying to staunch the purple blood that flowed from his neck.

Moon ducked the electrostick of the second Gray and stabbed him in the area where a human heart would be. When that didn't seem to slow him down, she slashed instead at the area on his head where she had seen the veins pulsing on HBH as he'd questioned her.

The second Gray dropped like a stone.

She pulled the electrostick from his still spasming hands and held it against another control panel. Gritting her teeth, she flipped the switch she had come to associate with pain. The familiar hum made her wince, but she held the electrostick firm as sparks flew around her, frying the controls for the weapons' station.

Sparks were still flying when the blade hit her square in the back, and she stumbled, nearly falling, as she turned. BH1 stared at her, his scarred mouth hanging open, obviously dumbfounded, as she twisted away from him, wrenching the knife from his hand. She could feel the metal grinding against the muscles in her back, but it was worth it to see a reaction on the Big Head's face as she swept her makeshift dagger across the veins on his skull. Violet blood sprayed over her, and she screamed in triumph.

An explosion rocked the room then, and she fell to her hands and knees. Red and purple blood pooled beneath her, and her hands slipped as another detonation shook the ground. She hit her cheek hard against the floor and lay winded. She scrambled in the blood, trying to get her elbows under her torso, to push herself up, to move. *Keep fighting!* But she had no strength left. Her hands were cold, numb.

Lifeless.

The word shook her. She heard Grays running by her, coming to investigate the fire that had started in the control room. With the knife protruding from her back and blood all around her, she must have appeared dead because they didn't stop to check her. *Maybe I am dead. Then I must be in hell because this shouldn't hurt so bad.* The thought made her want to laugh, but her breath was so shallow, she couldn't even manage a snort.

Cold crept up her arms to her chest. Sweat–chilly against her fevered skin—dripped from her nose and chin, but she couldn't move to wipe it away. All she could hear was her heartbeat, pounding a rhythm in her skull. Her sight had narrowed to the blood-slicked floor before her. A sudden terror gripped her. And a sudden regret for all the things she had left undone.

«Alex?»

«Brynn?»

«I love you, Alex. I know I don't say it . . .»

«Just hold on, Brynn. They're almost there. Just hold on a little longer.»

Moon closed her eyes. She was tired, so very tired. But she had done her job. She had played her part well. She'd always known she was an expendable spy, not a living spy.

Damn Suntzu. And damn Colonel Kim.

Still. She had done her job well.

«Moon? Brynn?»

She laughed silently to herself and struggled to find the energy to answer him. *God, I love him.*

«'In battle the enemy is engaged with the normal and defeated by the abnormal force. The abnormal force, skillfully handled, is like the heaven and earth, eternal; as the tides and the flow of rivers, unceasing; like the sun and moon, forever interchanging.' Bet they never expected this type of interchange between the Sun and the Moon, did they, love? We're about as abnormal as they come.»

She could hear tears across the link.

«You did it, Moon. You surprised them all. Just hold on a bit longer. Fleche is almost there.»

She exhaled softly. She knew a battle raged above her, but she felt so peaceful.

«I'm not going anywhere, my Sun. Nowhere at all.»

About the Authors

Celosia Crane is a spec-fic-writing, whiskey-loving lady with a passion for classic American muscle cars, and a penchant for hair flowers, leather jackets, and lipstick.

Weaving together themes of overcoming obstacles and discovering the strength within us all, her works include "The Ranger and the Greenwitch," "Drawing out the Poison," and "Elysium in the Snow."

You can follow her antics on Facebook at CelosiaCraneAuthor, on Twitter at CelosiaCrane, and on Instagram at The_Exotic_Aunt.

Kimberly Gail grew up in Kansas but has neither lived on a farm nor been swept away to a magical land by a tornado. She does craft magical worlds that she lovingly transforms into words through her writing.

She is mother to two newly minted adults and a highly opinionated teenager whom she is currently homeschooling. She also wrangles a small horde of animals, including a lazy but lovable puggle, an extremely self-important cat, and a baby dragon (of the bearded variety).

Her published works include "Amautalik and the Wolf" and "A Satyr's Lament." Follow her on Instagram at kimberly_gail_a_writers_life, on Facebook at AuthorKimberlyGail, and at kimberlygail.com.

About the Author

Hayley Green is a writer, avid reader, music lover, chocoholic, life-long learner, office supply collector, and organization and productivity buff.

Her love of reading, out of which writing grew, began before she remembers. Both were an extension of playing pretend and gave her creative imagination an outlet. Now, she channels her creative energy into cofounding *Write of Passion* as editor in chief, coleading the Write Away feedback group, and running daily word sprints. She can always be found in the middle of working on several writing projects at once, reading at least five different books and magazines, and going to school for a degree in creative writing.

You can follow her on Facebook or Twitter at HayleyGAuthor, at coffeehousewriters.com, and on her blog at hayleygauthor.com.

Kristine Haecker has been a prison guard, a grocery store checker, and an insurance agent, and she currently spends her days beating Excel into submission. All these experiences provide plenty of material for funny fiction from the real world. She primarily writes full-length beach-read novels and is expanding into short stories in fantasy and sci-fi. Her creative nonfiction has been published in *Creatives Rising* and upcoming *Write of Passion*.

She shares a fixer-upper in southern Wisconsin with her amazing husband and their two fur babies, Ripley and Tosh. When she isn't working on a story, she spends her time bingeing NCIS with her husband, playing with the fur babies, crocheting baby hats, going out to eat far too often, and cheering on the Green Bay Packers!

Shannon McRoberts writes epic fantasy and urban fantasy books while living in the rolling hills of Kentucky. Shannon is a lover of all kinds of fantasy but enjoys watching her collection of favorite shows, including Xena, Buffy, Firefly, Fairy Tail, Game of Thrones, and Farscape. When she's not busy taking care of her family, binge watching Netflix, or making fantasy art, Shannon is at her computer weaving myths and magic featuring women of grit and steel.

Follow her on Facebook at ShannonMcRobersOfficial, on Instagram at shannon_mcroberts, and on Twitter at obsidianpoet. Visit her website at. shannonmcroberts.com or shor.by/smcroberts.

Finn O'Malley is an elemental goddess who loves writing, crystals, and daydreaming about her next meal. She lives in northern Utah with her human husband, two lovable teenagers, and two cat overlords on the hunt for adventure, world domination, and wet food. When she is not in her garden growing human-sized bushels of herbs, you can find Finn sitting on a mountaintop practicing yoga or penning witty urban fantasy adventures for humans who need a break from reality.

Follow her on Facebook at FinnOMalleyauthor and on Instagram at finn.omalley.author, or you can visit her website at finnomalley.com.

About the Author

Leo Otherland is a dreamer, martial artist, and lover of all things strange and unordinary, from the arctic north woods of Wisconsin. This elusive scribbler acquired his passion for weaving stories of dark and broken things through a childhood spent huddling in books and dodging the unfriendly spirits residing in the haunted house he called home for several years.

Currently, Leo is doodling out a series of dark, dystopian fantasy novels and various short pieces in a very ordinary apartment, hidden away somewhere unobtrusive. During the slight occasions he is not writing, this finicky, unrepentant otaku enjoys reading web comics, watching anime, and playing JRPGs. And while it's rare to catch this skittish pensmith out in the daylight, his published works can be found in Creatives Rising and Write of Passion. The author himself can be located on Facebook at Leo Otherland - Author.

D. Marie Prokop enjoys stories with riveting adventures, spiritual insights, and enlightening cultural or social critiques. She is also a singer-songwriter and avid fiber artist / knitter. Born and raised in Pennsylvania, the former Yankee now resides in Houston, Texas, along with her loving family, their feisty cats, her beloved ukulele, and much, much yarn.

Follow her on Facebook at daysoftheguardian, on Instagram at dmarieprokop, on Twitter at anotherfolksie, and on Pinterest and YouTube at Diane Prokop. Visit her website at dmarieprokop.com.

Jess Reece was practically born with a pen in her hand. At the age of four, she wrote her first story about a dog who took a ride on an alien spaceship to the moon. As a teen and young adult, she won various local writing awards for her poetry and short fiction.

Jess's goals are to draw her readers into worlds as real to them as they are to her and to have them fall in love with the characters they get to know.

You can follow Jess on Facebook at JessReeceAuthor, on Twitter at jessreeceauthor, and on Instagram at jessreece_authorartist. You can also visit her website at jessreece.com.

Theda Vallee is an author of fantasy and urban fantasy, with occasional forays into post-apocalyptic sci-fi. She lives in the Pacific Northwest with her husband, two sons, three cats, and two yappy pups.

Living in a place where the sun never shines, she channels rain-induced delirium into creating fierce independent heroines who kick ass and take names. Her obsession with mythology and folklore can be seen as she often interweaves known legends into her vibrant worlds, though always with a distinctly Theda twist.

When she's not writing, you can find her hiking, reading everything she can get her hands on, and traveling to distant locales in search of snacks.

Theda is currently working on the third book of her Violetta Massoni Series. You can follow Theda to find out how to nab her other works and receive updates for everything that's coming: on Facebook at thedavallee and on her website at thedavallee.com.

About the Author

Deana Rose Wilson is a self-proclaimed weaver of fantasy. Born to a family of eight children living in a Montana town so small it boasted only a bar and a post office, she soon discovered books and writing as an outlet for her creative nature.

She earned her BA in creative writing from SNHU, minoring in screenwriting and history. Her published work includes "Fragmented," featured in *The Penmen Review*, and "Treason of Asphodel," featured in *Write of Passion*. With the help of a houseful of cats and kids, she is completing her high fantasy trilogy while doing research for several other novels.

You can follow her on Twitter at PhoenixRose18, on Instagram at deana.r.wilson, and on Facebook at Deana Rose Wilson, Author.

Amanda Mills Woodlee is a mediocre guitar player, "the best substitute teacher ever" (according to students she totally didn't bribe with candy), and the worst at turning in library books on time. She loves languages and speaks English, Spanish, French, and GIF. Travel and snacks are essential to her writing process. She is currently working on a series of short stories and her first novel. Amanda and her husband, Ryan, live in eastern Oregon with their cat and four chickens, who all run when she tries to hug them. You can find her portfolio and blog at amandamills woodlee.wordpress.com. Follow her on Facebook at Amanda Mills Woodlee - Author for writing updates, the occasional meme, and to ask her what color your birthday is.